Penric
and the
SHAMAN

Penric
and the
SHAMAN

— ❧ —

**A FANTASY NOVELLA
IN THE WORLD
OF THE FIVE GODS**

— ❧ —

Lois McMaster Bujold

SUBTERRANEAN PRESS 2017

First Hardcover Edition

ISBN
978-1-59606-815-5

Subterranean Press
PO Box 190106
Burton, MI 48519

subterraneanpress.com

I

IVE GODS, BUT vultures were huge when seen at this distance.

The bird cocked its pale head on its sinuous neck, peering at Inglis like a nearsighted old man, as if uncertain whether he was its enemy or its...breakfast, judging by the graying of the scudding damp sky overhead. It shuffled back and forth, its pantaloon-feathers stirring on its legs as it raised one talon-tipped foot and contemplated its dilemma. The hooked yellow beak seemed to take aim. Inglis opened his parched mouth and gusted a harsh hiss, like the fire in a blacksmith's forge when the bellows blew. The bird skipped back a pace, raising vast brown wings, as if it were a villain in a play swirling his cloak just before declaiming his defiance to fate.

Fate, it seemed, had Inglis at bay now. Run to ground. He scratched at that hard ground with a gloved hand, leather cold and stiff, but grubbed up only snow. Not enough light yet to see if there was much blood on it. The steep vale he had climbed out of last night was a shadowed gulf, the ice and the rocks a mosaic of white and black streaks, the scrubby trees vague claws. His head ached abominably. He had thought that a freezing man was supposed to go numb, but his trapped leg continued to throb. One last heave failed to shift anything. Angled downward on the slope, he had no strength left to pull himself upright and try to get some better leverage.

The vulture hopped again. He wasn't sure what it was waiting for. Reinforcements? They contemplated each other for an unmeasured time.

A dog barked, getting closer. Not mere yaps, but deep woofs, as if sounding from a chest the size of a barrel. A sharper bark joined the first, and another. The vulture flapped and heaved itself into the air, retreating, but only as far as a nearby bare-branched tree, as the dogs rushed up. Surely he was hallucinating—there could be no Great Beast *here*, but the deep-voiced dog was the size and shape of a wolf, and the wolf in Inglis's blood seemed to sing out to it. It shuddered in canine ecstasy, licking his face, rolling in the snow and waving its paws in the air only to jump up and lick again, as the other two swirled around him, whining and yipping. *Do you imagine I am your god? No gods here...*

Voices.

"What is it?"

"Something dead, looks like. Arrow, you idiot beast! Don't *roll* in it, you'll stink up the hut fair fierce—again..."

"Oh. It's a man."

"Anyone we know?"

Shadowy shapes moved around him. Someone dragged off the dog, but with a menacing growl it wriggled free, then began nosing him again.

"...No. Traveler."

"What's he doing this far off the pass road?"

"Getting his fool self killed, looks like."

"He took this track, alone in the dark, in this weather? Practically qualifies him for a suicide, I'd say. The Bastard's bait for sure."

"Should we haul his carcass down to Whippoorwill? Might be a reward or something."

A thoughtful pause.

"Eh, nor there might not be, and where's the point to that? Collect the reward now, save steps. Strip him and let the carrion birds give him a sky burial. It can make no difference to him."

"Well, it's about time somebody gave us a god's-day gift…"

Ah. The vulture's reinforcements have arrived.

Hands, plucking at his clothes. "Good cloth. Good boots—help me shift these rocks, and I bet we can get both of them."

"Might have to cut off the smashed one."

The leg, or the boot? No, they'd want the boot. Maybe the leg…

"Riding boots. So where's his horse? Think he was thrown?"

"Figure we could find it? It might have a pack, with more goods."

"He'd have to have been leading it, on this slope. Might have slipped…stupid to try to climb in those boots." A pause. "I don't see it down below."

"It'd be dead meat if it were…get *off* him, Arrow, you fool dog!"

Hands at his belt. "There's a purse! …Ah, piss. Not much in it."

"Fancy knife hilt. Hey, think those're real jewels?"

A snort. "Martensbridge glass, maybe."

They pulled at the sheath, trying to tug it free. Inglis's eyes unglued; he reached deep and found his last reserves, flinging his voice like a javelin: **"Don't touch my knife."**

A mad scramble back. "Bastard's teeth, he's still alive!" The lesser dogs went into paroxysms, barking wildly, and had to be beaten off him. The great dog went flat, ears and tail down, whimpering, licking his face and neck with abject servility. But the hands that had been tugging at his knife did not resume their attempted scavenge. *Sacrilege.* His powers, it seemed, had not wholly deserted him in craven company with his hope, faith, and courage.

"Father and Mother. *Now* what do we do?"

The very question that had been plaguing him for five hundred miles. Scraping for the last residue of truth left in him, he got out, **"Take me home."**

He wept, he thought, but he no longer cared who saw it. Perhaps the gray dawn was false, because the world around him darkened once more.

II

"**I**'M *BORED,*" WHINED Desdemona. "Bored, bored, bored."

Penric, as soon as he regained control of his lips from her, smiled down at the page across which his quill was carefully making its way. "Destroy a flea."

"We slew every flea in the palace precincts weeks ago. And all the lice as well."

"And I'm sure everyone here would be grateful to you," murmured Pen, "if they knew." He had learned early on in his association with his demon, which had gifted him with the powers, though not yet the learning, of a Temple sorcerer, to be *discreet* about the deployment of their magics. He deployed his quill in the setting down of the next three words in Darthacan, glanced up at the volume in the Wealdean tongue he was copying, and translated the next line in his head, cross-checking to be sure it *was* the next line, and not one up or down from it. He'd ruined not a few pages by that inattention.

He pressed his lips closed to prevent interruptions while he unloaded the complex medical phrase, then rolled his shoulders and stretched. "Your part will come soon," he said tranquilly. "Just three more lines and this page is done. You shall like that."

"It was only diverting the first hundred times. After that, it was as bad as worms."

Desdemona, formerly, had been the possession of a Temple physician-sorceress of the Mother's Order, devoted to medicine and the healing arts. Two such women, actually, in her long succession of riders. Which was where she had picked up her mastery of the Darthacan tongue, passing it in turn to him, and of medicine as it related to sorcery, in which Penric was...making slower progress.

"I shall not make you treat people's worms."

"You made us treat *bookworms.*"

Penric arranged another sentence in his head, and studiously ignored her till it was transferred. She did not try to interrupt, having learned by experience that however droll fouling his lines might seem to a demon of disorder, it just sent him around to start over at the beginning, and then she had to endure her tedium twice as long.

At her next chance, she said, "At least ask the princess-archdivine if we can ride courier for her again this week."

"Des, it's *snowing*." He glanced up at the fine glass window of his tiny, but private, work chamber on the palace's fourth floor, which let the light in and kept the vile weather out. In his not-that-long-ago youth at Jurald Court, his family's home at the feet of the great mountains that bounded the Cantons on the north, he'd been sent out in the snow to hunt or check the trap lines. Sitting indoors with a blanket over his lap, lifting nothing heavier than a feather, was *much* nicer, even as he'd discovered that the small muscles of the eyes and hands could get just as fatigued as big ones.

Last line. He sat up, read the page down once and up from the bottom once, matching it almost line-by-line to the original—Darthacan was a fluffier, if more structurally logical, tongue than Wealdean—and rose to collect the next wooden printing plate from the stack.

He had devised this process while studying at the Bastard's Seminary at Rosehall, adjunct to the great university in that Wealdean town. Poor scholars had to rent, and share, their frightfully expensive books, which had led to much brangling over turns, a couple of memorable fistfights, and one stabbing. Which Pen could never mix into because it would have been *unfair*, not to mention that few fellow students, once they learned of his sorcerous-if-untrained status, challenged him...

"...more than once," Des murmured smugly.

Des was getting disturbingly good at reading his thoughts, these days. *Practice, I suppose.* He was a bit peeved that the process did not seem to be reciprocal, though he had certainly grown able to sense her moods—*so many, many moods*—and had become almost unthinkingly fluent in their silent speech. When they were alone, he tried to let her chatter on aloud with his mouth as much as she pleased, which seemed to help keep her in a good humor. Bad idea when *not* alone, since their conversations all took place in his voice. To the confusion, and a few times violent offense, of their auditors.

He pulled the next prepared wooden plate off the stack at the end of his worktable, and carefully arranged his new page face-down across it. As habitually as when sitting down to dinner, he blessed the work with the tally of the gods: touching his forehead for the Daughter of Spring, his lips for the Bastard, his navel for the Mother of Summer, his groin for the Father of Winter, and spreading his hand over his heart for the Son of Autumn. And then tapped his thumb twice more against his lips, for luck. Sitting up straight, he said, "Ready, Des?"

"You hardly *need* me for this, anymore," she griped, but flowed into alignment with him nonetheless.

He passed his hand above the plate. A stink of wood rot and burning arose from it, along with a puff of steam mixed with smoke. His hand heated, pleasantly taming its cramping. His carefully calligraphed page grayed into ash.

He took up his brush and whisked away the ash and crumbs. Raised upon the surface was left a perfect mirror replica of his page, ready to turn over to the palace printer for making anything from a few dozen to hundreds of copies. The work would have taken an ordinary woodcarver the better part of a week, and wouldn't be nearly so fine. He could produce ten plates a day, and it was only that slow because he'd not yet figured out how to perform it with anyone's writing but his own.

The trick of it was in the destruction of the handwritten page, so that there was no net gain in order. Uphill, creative magic was costly; downhill, destructive magic was cheap. What happened to the plate afterward in the hands of ordinary men did not seem to impinge on this demonic summation. He could do this all day long.

The princess-archdivine had been delighted with his new skill, when he'd first shown it to her, and now used him regularly for her official pamphlets. In between those interrupting assignments, he was permitted to get on with the task of his heart, reproducing Learned Ruchia's two-volume work on sorcery and medicine to be distributed to the Bastard's Order throughout the Cantons and the Weald—and, soon, Darthaca and Ibra. (And after that, perhaps Adria and far Cedonia? Des moaned in prospect.) And to which he had added a short epilogue detailing his new technique—*A Codicil by Learned Penric of Martensbridge, Sorcerer*, he had proudly headed it—which should multiply its effect yet further. He owed Ruchia that living memorial, he thought, for death-gifting him with her demon, however inadvertently.

Well, inadvertent from his point of view, hers, and her demon's. He was uneasily unsure about the intentions of the white god that she, and now he, served. Though so far, Penric seemed to have been let get on with his life free of holy molestation.

At a cautious knock at his workroom door, Pen called, "Enter."

A palace page in the blue tabard of a dedicat of the Daughter's Order poked her head in, though only a few wary inches. She jerked back and waved a hand before her nose, grimacing, as the smoky fug of Pen's labors wafted out into the corridor. "Learned Penric, sir. The princess-archdivine bids you attend upon her in her private cabinet."

"Now?"

"Yes, Learned."

Penric waved amiable acknowledgment. "Very good. I'll follow presently."

The girl whisked away, and Pen rose and set his tools in order.

Hurrah! said Des. *Something new? An outing? An airing…?*

"More chores, more likely." Pen closed his door and made his way down the corridor.

THE PRINCESS-ARCHDIVINES of the royal free town and hinterland of Martensbridge were, by law and long custom, appointees in the gift of the distant Hallow King of the Weald. The town's charter from him, and fealty to him, were what made it royal; the distance was what made it free, Penric suspected. Save for one or two lapses that they had managed to repair by strategic marriages, bribes, and a few armed clashes, the high house of kin Stagthorne had held onto the throne through the past several generations of elections. The current holder of the Martensbridge benefice had thus been, by the turning furrows of time, first daughter, then sister, then aunt to the succeeding kings.

Princess-Archdivine Llewen kin Stagthorne was now a slight, shrewd woman of sixty, who had carried out her duties to the Temple in this pocket palatine realm with the firm hand of a frugal housewife for some thirty years. As Penric knocked at the door to her private cabinet, one floor down from his own and adjacent to her chancellery, and was bade to enter, he found her dressed in the five-colored holy robes of her Temple office. Presumably she'd been caught either on the way to or from some ceremonial task. She was flanked as usual by her secretary, a woman of like age—and shrewdness—in the silks and linen and fine woolens appropriate to the palace precincts.

A strange man was also present, not nearly so finely clad. Above middle height, broad-shouldered, fit; perhaps thirty years of age? Brown hair, gray eyes. Face and hands red and chapped with cold; recently shaved but not, given his road-reek, recently bathed; riding boots cursorily cleaned of mud. Pen might have taken him for some urgent courier, but for the distinctive gray doublet with the brass buttons peeking out from beneath his thrown-back black cloak.

What's a Wealdean Grayjay doing here?

The man eyed him in turn, then palpably dismissed him. Penric advanced to kiss the archdivine's ring, held out perfunctorily to his inky fingers, and murmured, "How may I serve you, Your Grace?"

"Well, let us find out. Pull up a chair, Penric." She nodded to the wall, where a few stools for favored visitors or supplicants were lined up. Unfavored ones were kept standing. The Grayjay had already been granted one, and the secretary another; the princess-archdivine occupied her carved seat, perhaps not accidentally reminiscent of a throne, and the only one supplied with a cushion. Supplicants were not encouraged to linger, not out of any high-nosed pride on the princess's part, but because there were always other supplicants waiting.

Llewen went on mildly, "How goes your latest translation?"

"Well, Your Grace. Another two weeks of *uninterrupted*"—Penric made sure to emphasize that last word; Desdemona snickered silently—"work should see it ready to send out into the world after its sister volumes. I'm starting to think about its Ibran-language edition. Some recent medical texts in that tongue would be useful for reference, if they might be obtained for me. Helvia and Amberein gave me the Wealdean and Darthacan terminology, but Aulia of Brajar was no physician. And also, she may be out of date."

The strange man's hand clenched in impatience upon his knee. *"Your Grace..."* squeezed out between his lips, protest constricted by politeness, or perhaps the prudence of a man who hadn't yet had his wish granted.

"Ah," said the princess. "Permit me to introduce Senior Locator Oswyl, agent of the Father's Order in Easthome. He is here, he tells me, on a mission of close pursuit, complicated by some very peculiar aspects, for which he earnestly begs the support of a sorcerer."

Senior Locator was a title of a Temple Inquirer of middle rank; not the lowly man-at-arms of a mere Locator, nor the heights of an Inquirer or, more dizzyingly, Senior Inquirer, who were normally learned divines, but something betwixt and between. Although the name of his Order's home chapter, from the royal capital itself, added some tacit clout. Penric sat up, interested, and offered the man a friendly smile and a little wave of his fingers. He did not smile back.

"And this is Penric, my sorcerer," Princess Llewen went on, with a nod Pen's way.

Oswyl's eyes widened. In a voice of unflattering surprise, he said, "*That's* your court sorcerer? I was expecting someone...older."

And better dressed, perhaps? Penric was very fond of his hard-earned white robes of the Bastard's Order, and wildly proud of his shoulder braids marking him as a divine and a sorcerer, but he had quickly learned not to wear them while at work. At least not when yoked with a demon of disorder with a questionable sense of humor. As a result, most days he went about the palace precincts looking the tattered clerk Oswyl had evidently taken him for. Since the palace denizens knew who he was by now, this was not usually a problem. He could turn himself out as a showy, and laundered, ornament to the court well enough when someone gave him warning...

Thinking of his incomplete translation, Pen stifled his leaping curiosity and offered, "You could try Learned Tigney of the Bastard's Order on Stane Street. He is the master and bailiff of all Temple sorcerers in this archdivineship." Not that this secretive company numbered many. Nor did that number include Penric, who owed fealty directly to the princess-archdivine in return for his late schooling.

"I started with Tigney. He sent me *here*," growled the Grayjay, sounding frustrated. "I told him I needed someone *powerful*."

"I trust," murmured the princess, "you do not judge so quickly by appearances in your inquiries, Locator."

Oswyl went a little rigid, but swallowed any attempt at answering this observation, *yes* or *no* being equally hapless choices.

Feeling faintly sorry for the man—he'd run into the sharp side of the princess's tongue himself a time or two, though never without having earned it—Penric offered peaceably, "So what do you need this powerful sorcerer for, sir?"

The princess waved her beringed hand. "Tell the tale again, Locator. With a bit more detail this time, if you please. If something so dangerous has entered my lands, I need to understand it."

Oswyl took a long breath, of a man about to recount the same story for, by Pen's guess, the third time in a day. At least it ought to be well-practiced. He at last addressed Penric directly: "What do you know of the Wealdean royal shamans?"

Penric sat back, or aback. "Not...a great deal. I've never met one in person. Their society is engaged in an attempt to recover something of the Old Weald forest magics, thought to be stamped out in the conquests of Great Audar. Except brought under the disciplines of the Temple, this time."

The Darthacan conquest of the Weald had taken three hard-fought generations, five hundred years ago; three generations later, Audar's empire had all fallen apart again in internal discord. But when the Darthacan tide receded, the Temple remained, and the old forest tribes, shattered and scattered as much by the passage of time and the progress of the world as by Darthacan arms, never reestablished themselves. Why the restored, if much changed, Wealdean hallow kings had sponsored this antiquarian revival when they had perfectly good Temple sorcerers at their disposal, Penric did not know, although the interested scholar in him felt a sneaking approval.

"The shamans' magic is a human creation, or at least, rising from the world instead of descending, or escaping, from a god as demons do," Penric went on. "In the old forests, tribal shamans were said to invest their warriors with the spirits of fierce animals, to endow them with that strength and ferocity in battle. The making of a shaman partook of this, only more so. The spirits of animals were sacrificed into others of the same kind, generation after generation, piled up until they became something more, Great Beasts. Invested at last into a person, the spirit of such a creature brought its powers to him not"— he cleared his throat—"not unlike the way a demon of the white god does for a sorcerer. Despite the very different origins of the gifts."

Humph, said Desdemona, but did not contradict this.

As Penric drew breath, the princess held up a stemming hand. "Penric is quite fond of reading, and will happily share all he learns. But perhaps not all at once? Go on, please, Locator."

The Grayjay pressed his forehead, as though it ached, and grimaced. "Right. The first the Father's Order at Easthome was told of this case was after that mess at the funeral, which was late off the mark. We should have been called out when they first found the body. Howsoever. I was dispatched to investigate and report on a suspicious death at the estate of one of the minor branches of the kin Boarford family, about ten miles outside of the capital. Not home of the earl-ordainer, thankfully, although for that I suppose they would have sent a more senior man.

"As I—eventually—worked out the chain of events, one of the scions of the family, a young man with military ambitions named Tollin kin Boarford, had purchased a wild boar captured alive from some hunters. He'd kept it for some weeks in a sty on the estate. His older brother thought that he had plans for some boar-baiting show, because instead of making any attempt to tame it, he teased it to make it wilder. Although I suppose either plan would have been equally stupid. But when Tollin was found one morning in the sty, shirtless and with his belly ripped open, and the boar bled dry with a knife in its throat, it seemed to the servants and family death by plain misadventure. The boar was butchered and fed to the dogs. Tollin's body was washed and wrapped and made ready for his funeral rites at the old family temple on the estate, conducted by the local divine.

"Which was where everything went wrong, because none of the funeral animals signed that any god had taken up his soul, not the Son of Autumn, which would have been expected, not the Bastard, nor any other. As far as his family could tell, he had become a sundered ghost, and no one knew why. The divine, *finally*, sent for help."

But instead, they got this Grayjay, Desdemona quipped. Penric pressed his lips closed.

"There was not much to see in the sty, and the boar was eaten by then, but I did, with some argument, get the family to allow me to unwrap and examine the body. Where I was apparently the first to notice that, in addition to the ghastly goring of his abdomen, there was a slit of a knife wound just under his left breast. Shifting the event from misadventure to murder."

"Huh," said Pen, impressed.

"At that point, I reexamined the knife, and determined that it was not only too wide to have made the wound, it was too wide to fit in Tollin's belt sheath. Not his blade at all. And after a search of the sty, its environs, and pretty much the whole estate, no other knife of the right dimensions was found. Carried off, it seemed, by whoever had stabbed him to the heart."

Huh, said Des, less unimpressed. She seized Pen's mouth to inquire, very much in Learned Ruchia's cadences, "Could you tell which injury came first, the knife wound or the goring?"

Oh, now that's an interesting question, Pen commented, deciding to forgive her for the unauthorized interruption, not least because Oswyl glanced across at him with a shade more respect.

"I could not. I'm not sure it would have been apparent even if I had been able to see the body when it was first found. But I took the knife and my inquiry to Tollin's friends. None of them recognized the blade, but at last I learned that Tollin had also been comrades with a royal shaman, one newly invested with his powers. A younger son of the northern kin Wolfcliffs."

The princess nodded. "That branch of their kin has been noted for supplying royal shamans since Good King Biast revived the practices, a century before my birth. Or so it was when I last lived at the king's hall in Easthome."

The Grayjay nodded back. "It's still so. This shaman, Inglis kin Wolfcliff, was said by his friends to have been trying to court Tollin's sister, without much success. When I went looking for him, I discovered that he had vanished out of Easthome, without leave from his superiors, the day after Tollin's death. No one knew where or why. They did identify the knife found in the boar as a ritual sort, but with no signs of the uncanny on it.

"Which is when I persuaded *my* superiors to issue an order for Inglis's arrest. And the wherewithal to carry it out, which was harder to extract. Inglis seems to be an ordinary-looking fellow—middling stature, dark hair and eyes, early twenties—of which I found there is a vast brotherhood on the roads this season, none of them well remembered by anyone. Fortunately, he rode a fine flaxen mare, a gift from his family upon the occasion of his investiture I was told, which was noted by every ferryman and inn stable boy from the lower Stork to the Upper Lure all the way to the Crow. Which was where we found the mare, lamed, sold to an inn hoping to resell her to a breeder. And our quarry vanished into air."

Penric cleared his throat. "Knowing what you pursued, shouldn't your superiors at Easthome have requisitioned you a sorcerer before you started out?"

Oswyl's jaw tightened. "They did. A sorcerer, six royal guardsmen, and three grooms. Upon the Crow River Road, we had a...strong difference of opinion as to which way Inglis might have fled. Learned Listere held out for his having made for Darthaca or Saone, to the east, to cross the border out of any jurisdiction of the Weald. I thought north, if for the same reason, making for the mountain passes out of these hinterlands into Adria or Carpagamo."

The princess raised her chin. "If so, the shaman is out of his reckoning. The passes were blocked by snow a week ago. They don't normally open again until spring. Unless you think he outraced our late-autumn blizzards?"

Oswyl's lips unpressed unhappily. "From the Crow? If so, he would have had to be flying, not walking. My hope is to find him bottled up above your lake somewhere, stranded like a laggard merchant."

"So where is your Easthome sorcerer now?" Penric prodded.

"Halfway to Darthaca, I suppose," growled Oswyl. "And all the troop with him, as they refused to be divided."

That is a very determined Grayjay, Penric observed to Desdemona, *to follow his own line though his whole pack hares off without him.*

Or a typical devotee of the Father's Order, she returned, *with a rod up his fundament and an obsession with his own rightness.*

Who is judging by appearances now? Really, the man had just covered, what, four hundred miles between Easthome and Martensbridge, along muddy roads as winter whistled in, pushing ten men to ride as fast as a man alone. And losing his race and chase by very little margin. No wonder he seemed vexed.

Penric asked cautiously, "What exactly are the powers of this shaman, Locator? As you and your Order in Easthome understand them to be? If I am to be assisting you in this arrest?" *Or making it for you, sounds like.*

Oswyl turned out his chapped hands. "Shamans are said to have great powers of persuasion or compulsion—in the strongest form, to be able to lay a geas upon a person that can last for weeks. The weirding voice, they call it."

Penric's lips twitched. "Sounds as if the hallow king should be making them royal lawyers, not royal warriors."

This got him a grim glare from the Grayjay. *No jokes, right. Oh, well.*

"I am also told that this voice does not work on sorcerers. Or rather, does not work on their demons."

That is actually correct, murmured Desdemona. *Remind me to tell you of the one Ruchia met on one of her missions to Easthome, who tried to seduce her.*

Did he succeed?

Yes, but not for that reason…

With some difficulty, Penric wrenched his attention back to the Grayjay. *Later.* And very much not only for the salacious tale.

"It's unclear to me," continued Oswyl, frowning in untrusting speculation at Penric, "what happens should the weirding voice fail with the demon but work on the sorcerer."

I will save you, Penric! Desdemona promised, in a dramatic tone. *...Unless, like Ruchia, you should not care to be saved.*

That one, Pen ignored. "What else?" asked Pen.

"Like their ancestors, they are supposed to be savage and merciless in close combat."

Hence the six royal guardsmen, Pen supposed. Now on their way to Darthaca. How could he face down a desperate murderer possessing, presumably, trained martial skills, in a maniacal battle-frenzy? Not that Pen didn't possess certain powers of speed and evasion, not to mention distraction, in his own right, but...he thought perhaps he might take his hunting bow along. The one with the heavy draw and the really long range.

Sound thinking, said Des. *I should not in the least care to replace you with whatever stray passerby happened to be around if you became careless.*

When their person died, a demon, unbound by this dissolution, perforce jumped to another nearby. Temple rites for a dying sorcerer assured that the approved recipient would be prepared and standing ready. Alas that not every sorcerer died to schedule... *Could you jump to this shaman?*

No. He'd be full-up.

Huh. I suppose that would leave the Grayjay...

Desdemona shuddered, delicately.

Confident that his demon would do everything in her very considerable powers to keep him alive—and, Pen confessed to himself (*and us*, put in Des), stirred to keen curiosity by all this lurid tale—he straightened on his stool, preparing to volunteer the services that everyone here so clearly was about to ask of him. But the Grayjay was going on.

"There was one other task for the forest mages. That was to bring back the souls of their slain spirit-warrior comrades from the battlefield, to undergo certain cleansing rites necessary for them to go to the gods. To prevent them from being sundered and lost."

"I've read a little of that," said Penric. "Those were the banner-carriers, right? As ghosts are some-times bound to a place, they would bind them to their banners, to carry away to safety. That was *real?*"

"I...maybe. The thing is..." Oswyl hesitated. "As signed or, more correctly, not signed by his funeral miracle, Tollin was taken up by no god. He might have refused the gods out of despair, or been refused by them, and been sundered. Doomed to dissolution as a fading ghost. Or worse, involuntarily polluted by some incomplete rite, prevented from reaching his god reaching for him." Oswyl grimaced at this sacrilege.

Pen had to agree with that sentiment. To murder a man was a crime. To deliberately sunder his soul from the gods, stealing not a life but that mysterious, eternal afterlife, was sin of the darkest, cruelest sort, a theft of unfathomable enormity.

"I requested a Temple sensitive to search the estate for any evidence of his lingering ghost. She found nothing. Well, not *nothing*, there were a few sad revenants faded beyond recognition, dozens or hundreds of years old. But the distraught sundered ghost of a freshly murdered man should have been livid in her Sight, she said. Tollin's soul simply was not there."

Oswyl drew a long breath. "As Inglis took nothing on his flight that he did not own, he is not accused of theft. I think that belief may be... mistaken."

Penric's jaw unhinged. "You think the man stole a *ghost?*"

Or should that be *abducted? Ravished away? Taken hostage?* This crime was going to need a whole new law devised to cover it. Just the sort of hair-splitting argument the Father's Order reveled in, Pen supposed.

Hang the Father's Order, murmured Des in new alarm. *There will be more fearsome Powers than the gray company with an interest in* this *pilferage…*

The princess-archdivine, too, was staring in amazement at the tight-lipped locator. Had he not ventured quite so far in his prior testimony to her? He stirred uncomfortably, making a truncated wave as if to distance himself from his own deduction, but then that hand clenched closed. "None of my superiors think so. But *I* do."

III

---

*T*O OSWYL'S RELIEF, the princess-archdivine took his tale seriously enough to gift him with both the loan of her court sorcerer, and of a small troop of her palace guards, local men of the Daughter's Order whose calling was to protect Temple property and pilgrims. To his frustration, the expanded party was not readied until the morning.

He'd used the time as well as he could, canvassing the lower town across the Linnet River where merchants and caravans stopped, and where the inns, taverns, smithies, saddlers, liveries, and other businesses catering to the trade of travelers were congregated. The docks and quays servicing the lake traffic were growing quieter with the advancing season, although the lake had not yet frozen over. But in neither venue was he able to unearth any sure report of a lone traveler matching his quarry's description.

The laggard winter sun was rising gray and gold as they cleared the town gates and at last took to the main road north, skirting the lake's western margin. It had stopped snowing, leaving no more than a finger's width of dirty white trampled on the half-frozen ruts. As the town fell behind and the long valley lake widened, Oswyl stared across doubtfully at the farther shore, dark against the dawn. All farm tracks and rugged scrubland climbing the heights on that side, he'd been told, a route unlikely to be chosen by a fugitive in a hurry. But what about a fugitive wishing to hide? For all that this realm had looked small on a map, it seemed much more spacious on the ground.

No, take it logically; search the most likely possibilities first, then the lesser. He stared between his horse's bobbing ears, and tried not to feel so tired.

Turning in his saddle, he checked their outriders, a sergeant-at-arms and four men, all looking sturdy enough bundled against the cold, then glanced aside at his new sorcerer. At least this one rode better than the last one, who had been a town-bred man of considerable seniority but also age and girth. This Penric looked a lean youth, with fine blond hair now tied back in a braid at his nape, and deep blue eyes whose cheer, at this hour, Oswyl found far more irksome than charming. It was hard to believe that he held the rank of a learned divine. Or the powers of a Temple sorcerer, either.

To top it off, the princess-archdivine had divided the purse for this venture, for which he was grateful, between the sergeant and the sorcerer, for which he was not. They were her own trusted men, to be sure, but just such a split in authority had been a chief source of infuriating delays in his ride from Easthome. The Temple remounts were a plain blessing, though, and he composed a prayer of thanksgiving in his mind to the Daughter of Spring for Her mercies, howsoever conveyed through Her prickly handmaiden the princess. Archdivines had seldom come Oswyl's way, princesses never; both combined in one person, who reminded Oswyl unnervingly of his most forcible aunt, had been daunting. Though her sorcerer had seemed entirely at his ease in her company, as if she were his aunt indeed.

Some ten miles down the road the cavalcade approached a handsome castle, built on an islet a little out from the lakeshore, that had been growing in Oswyl's eye and interest. As they drew even with it, Learned Penric twitched his horse aside and rode out on the causeway. The drawbridge was fallen in, its timbers blackened. The interior was shadowed, deserted and dismal.

Penric stared meditatively, then muttered, "Huh," and turned his horse back.

"What was this place? What happened to it?" Oswyl asked, looking over his shoulder as he followed.

"Castle Martenden. The clan of kin Martenden used to be something of a force in this region, for good or ill, but four years ago last spring the fortress was gutted with fire. Its lord had been charged with an, er, attempted murder, but fought his way free of the town guard and fled north over the mountains with a remnant of his men. He was reported to have raised a mercenary company in Carpagamo, but, happily, instead of returning to make trouble here, he took them on to the wars on the Ibran peninsula, where he may well have better hopes of restoring his fortunes."

The endemic wars against the Roknari Quadrene heretics in those far realms were a noted sink of landless men, both honorable ones and rogues. Oswyl nodded understanding. "But why hasn't it been repaired and put back into use by the town, to guard the road?"

"Tied up in litigation. Lord kin Martenden managed to be both attainted by the town council for his crime, and interdicted by the Temple for, er, certain impieties, so both claimed the spoils. The law courts of Martensbridge have been as good as a cockpit ever since. Townsmen take bets on the outcomes of the latest appeals."

Oswyl considered this tale, lips pursing. "Was he actually guilty of the crime charged, do you have any idea? Because...*interests* can have strange effects on such disputes." He frowned in speculation.

"Oh," said Penric airily, "I'm sure he was. There were warranted witnesses. And confessions."

The sorcerer then directed his attention to the hamlet on the opposite side of the road, and its shabby inn and alehouse, as a source of hot cider and information. While the troop took advantage of the former, Oswyl pursued the latter. Yes, the tapster opined, there might have been such a young man pass through a week ago, but many travelers refreshed themselves here, though few lingered, pushing on instead to the larger towns at the lake's head or foot. Not for the first time, Oswyl wished Inglis kin Wolfcliff had possessed the courtesy and foresight to be born with a large portwine birthmark on his face, or six fingers on his left hand, or grown to a giant of a man, or a dwarf, or had a limp or a stammer, or anything memorable at all.

"Do you think *you* will be able to identify the accursed man, should we ever come up to him?" Oswyl, exasperated, asked Penric as they mounted and headed north once more.

The youth looked introspective for a moment. "Oh, yes. If he's an invested shaman, Desdemona can't mistake him."

"And *who*," Oswyl went on, not less exasperated, "is this bloody Desdemona woman you keep going on about?" Wife? Sister? Leman? Not a member of this party, in any case.

Penric—*Learned* Penric, the gods help them all—blinked. "Oh! I'm sorry. I did not realize you had not been introduced. Desdemona is my demon." He smiled cheerily across at Oswyl.

"You *named* your *demon?*"

"Really, it was necessary. To keep all of her straight. She's quite a complicated person."

In Oswyl's theology, demons were not persons at all, but elemental forces of…un-nature. From the gods, or at least, from one god, but not by that reason holy. "I thought demons were fundamental chaos. Not capable of *being* anything."

"They all start out that way, it's true. Not anything at first. Rather like a newborn infant. But like an infant, they learn. Or perhaps copy. They learn from the people and the world around them, and they carry much of that learning along with them as they cascade down through time from master to master. Everything about them that might be called either good or evil comes ultimately from their human riders."

Oswyl frowned at this novel view. "I thought they were inherently destructive, and dangerous withal."

"Well, so they are, but destruction need not be inherently evil. It depends upon how cleverly it is deployed. When Desdemona was the possession of Learned Helvia, who was a physician, she destroyed stones of the bladder, a very painful condition I am told, and warts, and sometimes even tumors." He added after a distracted moment, "And worms, that were debilitating their victims. Though an apothecary's vermifuge could do that task as well."

If sorcerers were rare, physician-sorcerers were rarer still. "I have never met such a practitioner."

"I gather they are kept rather apart by the Mother's Order, to spare them for special tasks." After a thoughtful moment, he added, "Their sex, too, is something demons learn. Desdemona has been possessed by some ten women over time—plus the mare and the lioness—so she's grown quite feminine by now. She's an exceptionally old demon. It's rude to tell a woman's age, Penric!" His hand flew to his lips. "Uh, sorry. That was Des."

"It…talks? With your mouth? And yet it is not ascendant?"

"She. Yes, she does, and no, she's not. They can get quite chatty, among the ten of them. So if I say something strange, ah…it might not always be me. I should warn you of that, I suppose."

A sudden change in demeanor and speech was supposed to be one way an observer who was not a Temple sensitive could tell if a demon had ascended, seizing control of its rider's body for itself. But if the demon was leaking out *all the time*, how could it be discerned if such an emergency had occurred? Oswyl edged his horse slightly farther from the sorcerer's.

Penric piffled on, "Back at seminary I once sat down with a quill and paper and tried to work out her exact age, going back through all her riders one by one. Connecting them to some dated king's reign or public event whenever we could."

Reluctantly fascinated, Oswyl asked, "How do you keep them all straight? Or do you?"

Penric let his reins fall to his plodding horse's neck, held up both hands, and wriggled the digits, as if pleased to find them in place there. "Ten ladies, ten fingers. Very convenient."

"Ah," Oswyl managed.

"The Temple had planned to gift their star demon to another physician when Helvia died, but instead it jumped to a senior acolyte named Ruchia, who was of Martensbridge here. Oh, I see"—Penric blinked absently—"Helvia was *visiting* Martensbridge at the time. I'd wondered about that. Anyway, the Bastard's Order at Martensbridge not being slow off the mark, they promptly claimed Ruchia for themselves, and hurried her through the tutorials of a divine. In return, Learned Ruchia gave, er, extremely *varied* service to the Order and the Temple for the next forty years. She certainly seems to have traveled, in her duties. Which was how, when she had her fatal seizure of the heart some four years back, I came upon her on the roadside near Greenwell Town, and...here we all are."

"How old were you?"

"Nineteen."

Making him all of twenty-three, now. He still looked nineteen. Or, Oswyl might allow, twenty. At a stretch. "Were you some sort of precocious scholar, as a youth?"

"Not at all. I liked to read, but there weren't many books to be had in Greenwell."

"Yet you dashed through the learning for a divine in just four years?" It normally took six.

"Three. I came back here to the Princess-Archdivine's service last spring. You have to realize, I—we—had already been through the training for a divine four times already. In a sense. And twice for a physician. So it was more of a *refreshing*. I tried to talk the seminary's masters into granting me my rank fivefold on that basis, but they resisted my blandishments, more's the pity."

"I suppose...it was as if you already carried a tutor inside of you?" Which seemed like cheating, somehow.

Penric grimaced. "Mostly. Although Desdemona thought it was just hilarious never to help me out during my oral examinations. It would have been bad for you, Penric." His brows twitched up, and his mouth, down. "Ha-ha."

Was that last an interjection from the demon? The voice sounded faintly altered in cadence and accent from the strangely sunny young man's usual tones.

"That was Ruchia," Penric put in, confirming Oswyl's guess. "Desdemona speaks with her voice a lot. I don't know if it's because she is the latest and freshest, er, imprint, or held the demon longest, or simply had the strongest temperament. Time may have something to do with it. The first three women are almost impossible to tell apart, and I don't think it's just because they shared the Cedonian language. They may be melting together with age." He stared out over the lake, pewter gray and rippling bleakly in the chill wind blowing down from the distant mountain peaks shrouded with clouds. "Altogether, I calculated my demon is just over two hundred years old. I have noted," he added, "that the demon-generations are getting longer, as this tale goes on. I find that heartening, myself. I sometimes wonder what my...imprint will seem like, to the next person to inherit Desdemona."

"Your head seems very, uh, crowded," Oswyl offered at last, into the rather blighted silence that followed this.

"Very," said Penric. He brightened. "But at least I never lack for tales."

"I...wait. Now which was Desdemona, again?" The question he'd started this interrogation with, Oswyl dimly recalled. He kept his fingers curled firmly on his reins.

"That's my name for all of her together. Like a town council of ten older sisters who issue one edict. It also saves my running down several names every time I wish to address her, like my father shouting at his children."

"I...see." Oswyl's brows drew down. "The sorcerer I rode with from Easthome never told me anything like this." The dour fellow had not talked much at all, in fact.

"Perhaps his demon was younger and less developed. Perhaps he does not have a very cordial relation with it, if its prior riders were not happy men." Penric's lips twitched up, and his voice shifted a betraying hair. "Perhaps you never asked—Inquirer."

Oswyl hunched his shoulders and pressed his horse into a trot. They could not reach the next town soon enough. *And I am betting not only my mission, but maybe my life, upon this mad-brained sorcerer? Father of Winter, in this Your season, help me!*

IV

*I*NGLIS WOKE IN dimness, but not darkness. A bright square proved to be a small window on the wall of a hut, covered with parchment. On the opposite side, a rough stone fireplace gave off a red gleam and a few yellow flickers, like animal eyes peering out of a little cave. The walls were a mix of stone and logs, chinked with moss and mud. He lay tucked up in a nest of faintly reeky furs, on a floor of dirt scattered with crushed bracken. The big dog lay curled at his feet, sleeping, its paws loose and relaxed.

His boots and outer garments were gone, his chest bare. Convulsively, he felt at his waist, then sagged back down as his hand found his knife hilt. He still wore his belt and trousers. He had no memory of having arrived here, but he did have a dim recollection of someone feeding him warmed water, and of floating awake in darkness only to drown again. How much time had passed...?

And do you still have all your fingers and toes, fool? That was a question he might answer. He struggled up out of the furs—bear, sheepskin, others less identifiable. His hands were stiff and swollen, but not tipped white or scabbed black. His right leg was bruised dark purple from knee to bulging ankle; he couldn't tell if anything was broken, but it did not move well. Sprained, certainly. Three of his right toes oozed, as if burned. The left foot was no worse than his hands.

How much time lost? Had he missed all of yesterday? Anxiously, he sat up straight, squinted, and began the familiar count down the red scabs crisscrossing his arms. Twenty-five, the tally of his nightmare flight. Had it been twenty-five at last reckoning? *Yes.* Had he lost a day, failed to blood his knife, like a lazy farmer neglecting to feed his pig trapped starving in its pen? Had he lost...everything? He pulled the blade from its sheath, cradled it in his hands like a child, crooned anxiously. Extended his senses as painfully as he shifted his body. Oh bless, the faint warmth still hummed... he wasn't sure if he should thank any god for it. Or if any god would ever thank him. No telling. For twenty-five days, he had not dared to pray.

Except for this. He counted down the scabs, trying to recall which arm he had used last. He'd alternated strictly, to give time to heal between assaults. Infection was a constant risk. He should whet the knife again soon, to keep it sharp and make this easier. His right hand was steadier just now; so, left arm. He composed himself as well as he could, closed his eyes, and sliced: angled, shallow. He panted, waited for his head to stop swimming, the twist of nausea to settle. Opened his eyes again. Blood flow sluggish, but maybe if he squeezed there'd be enough that he wouldn't have to take a second—

The hut's door banged open, and he flinched worse than at the cutting. Blurry silhouettes swirled against the bright mountain air beyond. He blinked through tears more from the sharp pain of the light than the gash on his arm, and the figures resolved into a woman, sheepskin cloak bundled about her, carrying a small cloth sack and a copper pitcher, and a man in leathers wearing a sheepskin vest, fleece turned inward. The dog jerked alert and growled, but the growl trailed off in a few tail-thumps of recognition.

Seeing him sitting up, the woman said, "Oh, you're awake," but then, as she came closer, cried sharply, "What are you *doing?*"

He wanted to hide knife and arms beneath the furs, but he dared not stop this once started. "Stand back!" he commanded, and, as she made to swoop on him, **"Stand back."** The dog scrambled up, fur rising along its spine. The woman stopped abruptly, staring in dismay. The man's hand froze on the work-knife at his belt.

Whispering words under his breath that were supposed to help his focus, but really didn't just now, he stropped the knife blade up and down along his arm, coating it thoroughly in sticky red. Would it be enough to buy one more day? The faint hum seemed to strengthen. *Yes. Perhaps.* He wasn't sure but what a single drop would do the job as well, but he couldn't take chances. He held the knife in his lap, trying to protect it from his intruders' shocked gazes. When the blood smears turned brown and crumbling, all life sucked from them, he could clean the blade and hide it away once more.

The woman said tremulously, "I brought you food. And drink." She held up her burdens as if in evidence.

The man, scowling at Inglis, stepped in front of her. "Suppose you just put that knife away, fellow."

Did they think he threatened them? Inglis wasn't sure he could even stand up just now, let alone attack a person. His eye drawn by the pitcher, he raised the fur across his lap and slid the knife out of sight down next to his right thigh. He licked dry lips and set both hands out atop the cover, spread and still. He most certainly didn't want to frighten off that charitable young woman. Was the man's voice one of those he had heard in his daze upon the rockslide? Vulture, or rescuer? The dog sat back down.

"What were you doing with it?" asked the woman in suspicion, coming no nearer.

"I...it...it drinks blood." He wondered if that sounded as deranged to them as it did to him.

"All knives do," observed the man, his hand not leaving his own hilt.

Not like this one. "I drink drink," Inglis essayed hopefully.

"Travelers get dry in the mountains," said the woman, in a tone of careful placation. "They think because they are not hot, they are not thirsty."

"I...yes."

She circled wide around him to the hearth, collected a clay cup faintly familiar from last night, and filled it from the pitcher. She extended it to him with a long reach. He took it with a hand that shook, then both hands, and gulped down its contents, an unstrained barley water flavored with mint. Invalid stuff, far from a noble beverage, but it was warm, seeming both food and drink. He extended the cup back. "Please...?" He drained it three times before he stopped *guzzling*. He caught his breath and nodded thanks.

"Who are you—traveler?" asked the man.

"I, uh...Inglis k—" He cut off his too-famous kin name. "Inglis." *Oh. Should I have offered an alias?*

"Where were you bound?" asked the young woman. "Towards Martensbridge, or Carpagamo? Either way, you took a wrong turn."

"Pass from Carpagamo's closed," said the fellow, "Unless he was the last man to come in over it."

Inglis shook his head. He followed the dog's interested gaze to the cloth sack. Gingerly, the woman held it out to him. His clumsy fingers found it contained generous lumps of some soft white cheese, sheep or goat, captured between parsimonious slices of heavy barley-and-oat bread, and strips of dried smoked meat of uncertain origin. Venison, perhaps. Inglis, after a moment's hesitation, tore into it as if he were a wolf indeed.

After allowing the first couple of frantic swallows, the man asked, "Where's your horse?"

Around his mouthful Inglis answered, "Left her lame on the Crow Road. Then I walked."

"Oh." The man's mouth pursed in disappointment.

It came to Inglis that the young woman must have prepared this repast for him, with her own hands. He eyed her more closely over his chewing. Her face was mountain-broad, lips and cheeks rouged only by cold, her body work-lean; her youth lent her a passing prettiness. The fellow was not much older. Hunter, shepherd? Both? Up here, all men put their hands to all tasks, as the turning seasons ordered them. The two shared the light hair and blue eyes of this mountain stock, close kin surely.

"Who are you?" Inglis asked in turn after his next swallow. "Where is this place?"

The woman smiled hesitantly at him. "I'm Beris. That's my brother Bern."

Bern offered more reluctantly, "This is the summer grazing camp for Linkbeck, the village in the valley. Our hunting camp in winter."

So, he'd not traveled quite so far back in time as the place's crude look suggested. Not to the world of Great Audar's era, when these mountain tribes had held their high fastnesses against the invaders as the Wealdean forest tribes had not. Or maybe the Darthacans had taken one look at the damp precipitous country and decided they didn't want it that much. The Temple's invasion in these lands, replacing the old ways with the new, had been a slower process, more a gradual weeding out than a violent burning over. With a chance, a hope, if not a prayer, that they'd not uprooted everything...

No. He eyed the great dog, its furry triangular ears pricked as it tracked the progress of the meat strips to his mouth. *A certainty.* "That dog. Who owns it?"

"Arrow is Savo's beast," said Beris. "Had him from his uncle Scuolla this past autumn."

The dog lay down on its belly, wriggled up to Inglis, and shoved its head under his left hand. No pup, but a full-grown animal, mature—middle-aged and dignified, after a fashion. Absently, Inglis scratched it behind the ears. Tail thumping, it whined and licked at his bloodied arm.

"He seems to think he's your dog, now," said Bern, watching this play through narrowed eyes. "Hasn't left your side since we brought you in. Why is that—traveler?"

"Was Savo with you when you found me?"

"Aye, we'd gone out hoping for red deer. I'm not sure you were a fair trade, since we can't skin or eat you."

They'd seemed willing enough to skin him; Inglis trusted they would have stopped short of the eating, yes. But there had been no shaman among the hunters, or they would surely have recognized each other, and this conversation would be very different. So, not Savo.

"That knife," said the brother, Bern, looking at him sideways. "Are those real jewels? I bet Churr not."

Inglis had never imagined they might not be real. He drew out the knife and stared at it. The slim eight-inch blade was hafted in walrus ivory; he could feel the echo of old life in it when he held it in his hand. The beautifully curving hilt widened to an oval at the end, capped with gold, flat face holding small garnets, one gone missing in some past time and not replaced. They encircled a cabochon-cut red stone he guessed might be a ruby. *Tooth and blood, how fitting.* His blood on the steel had darkened and dried already, its life sucked in as ravenously as he'd just wolfed down hard bread and cheese. He set about rubbing off the residue on his trouser leg. "I suppose so. It was an heirloom."

The silence in the room grew a shade tighter. He glanced up to find a disquieting stew of curiosity, avarice, and fear simmering in his watchers' faces. But...they had brought him in off the mountain, and given him food and drink. He owed them warning.

"Why do you, uh, give it your blood?" asked Beris warily. "Is it, that is, do you think it's a magic knife?"

Inglis considered the impossibly complicated truth, and the need to quash that avarice before it created trouble—*more* trouble—and finally settled on, "It is accursed."

Bern drew breath through his teeth, half daunted, half dubious.

Beris's gaze tracked up and down the scabs on his arms. "Couldn't you feed it, I don't know, animal blood?"

"No. It has to be mine."

"Why?"

His lips drew back in something not much like a smile. "I'm accursed, too."

The pair excused themselves rather swiftly, after that. But they left the food and barley water. Arrow declined to follow, though invited with an open door, soft calls, chirps, a whistle, and firm commands. Bern circled back as if to grab the dog by its ruff and drag him, but, at Arrow's lowered head and glower, thought better of the plan. The door closed behind them.

Like most people, they underestimated the keenness of Inglis's hearing.

"What do you make of him now?" asked Beris, pausing a few paces beyond the hut.

"I don't know. He talks like a Wealdman. I think he must be out of his head."

"He wasn't very feverish. Do you think he might be uncanny? Dangerous?"

"Mm, maybe not to us, the shape he's in right now. Perhaps to himself. Churr could inherit that knife he coveted so much after all, if he goes from chopping up his arms to cutting his own throat."

"Why would a fellow *do* such a thing?"

"Well, mad." (Inglis could *hear* the shrug.)

"His voice was very *compelling*, did you feel it? It gave me the shivers."

"Mother and Daughter, Beris, don't be such a girl." But the mockery was tinged with unease.

"I *am* a girl." A considering pause. "He might be handsome, if he smiled."

"Don't let Savo hear you say that. He's already annoyed enough about his dog."

"I am not Savo's *dog*."

Siblings indeed, for then he barked at her, and she hit him, and their squabbling voices faded out of even Inglis's earshot.

He coaxed the dog up under his arm with a bribe of smoked meat. Hugged him in, stared into the clear brown eyes, then closed his own and tried to *sense*. The animal's spirit-density was almost palpable, hovering just beyond his present crippled reach. How many generations of dogs were poured into this Dog? Five? Ten? More than ten? How many generations of men had cultivated it? This could be a dog to make a shaman, immensely valuable.

And who was Scuolla, to give such a treasure away? Was the man an illicit hedge shaman, had he *made* Arrow? Intended this nephew Savo for his secret apprentice? Or was he unknowing of what he'd possessed? Horrifying, that he might be unknowing.

Appalling hope, that he might be wise.

"As soon as I'm on my feet," he told the dog with a little shake, "let's go find this ungrateful old master of yours, eh?"

Arrow yawned hugely, treating Inglis to a waft of warm dog-breath entirely lacking in enchantment, and rolled over like a bolster against Inglis's side.

V

*P*ENRIC'S PARTY CAME to the town of
Whippoorwill, at the head of the lake, in
the early winter dusk. It was half the size of the more
successful Martensbridge, and a bit resentful of the
fact, but still fivefold larger than Greenwell Town of
Penric's youth. Even the anxious Grayjay made no
suggestion that they press on any farther this night.
At the local chapter of the Daughter's Order, which
lay under the princess-archdivine's direct rule, they
found crowded, but free, lodgings.

Then Oswyl made the first practical use of the
troop that had trailed them by sending them all out,
severally, to ask after their quarry in the inns and taverns of the town. He didn't mention brothels aloud;

Penric was unsure if they were tacitly implied, if he thought the fleeing murderer would make no use of them, or if he was simply respectful of the guardsmen's oaths to the Daughter's Order. All business in Whippoorwill was settling down to merely local traffic as the high roads to the northern coast countries closed off for the season.

Penric and Oswyl had just finished eating at the tavern of their choice where, alas, no one remembered a dark-haired and dark-eyed Wealdean heading north alone in the past week, though any sensible fellow attempting the passes this late might have joined one of several parties and who would have noticed him then? Oswyl was rubbing his eyes in pain at this prospect when one of the guardsmen, Baar, came back. "I think I may have found something, sirs..."

With open relief but guarded hope, Oswyl followed at his heels down the streets, Penric trailing, to a lesser inn just off the main north road. Its air was homey and shabby, and it mainly served frugal local countrymen.

"Oh, aye," said the tapster, when Oswyl had lubricated the man's tongue with a pint of his own ale, and his purse with three more all around for their company. "Don't know if he's the man you seek, but certainly a well-set-up young fellow with dark hair and eyes. That describes half the Darthacans on the roads—"

Oswyl nodded rueful agreement.

"—but this one spoke with a Wealdean accent, and not lowborn. I thought he must be a scholar, because he said he wanted tales, as he was writing a book. Collecting them, see."

Oswyl's eyebrows went up. "What sort of book?"

"Old tales of the mountains, uncanny ones. Campfire tales, children's stories, ghost stories. Not saints' legends, much. He was especially interested in tales of magical beasts."

"Did he get any from you?" asked Penric.

"Oh, aye! It was a busy night." The tapster looked around mournfully at his current near-empty premises. "After he bought a round or two, I think he might have got enough for half his book right here."

"Did he seem especially intent about any particular tales? Ask more questions?"

"He seemed quite pleased to get the fellows going on about rumors of uncanny animals being bred up in the high valleys."

Penric came more alert. "Do you mean, um, current rumors, not just old stories? What are they?"

"Well, there's supposed to be a man up the Chillbeck who raises specially smart dogs, very prized by the local shepherds and hunters. I've met some right smart mountain dogs, though, so's I don't know as there's anything more to it than tales and bragging."

"Did he say anything about following those rumors to their source?" asked Pen.

"No, can't say as he did. He didn't say much about himself, come to think. Contented just to listen, y'know."

Oswyl put in, "Did he ask much about Carpagamo, Adria, the passes? Anything about how to get to the north coast?"

"A man hardly needs to ask about the passes this time of year—folks scarce talk about anything else, always hoping for a late thaw and one last chance to get through. But no, I don't recollect as he did. He seemed tired. Went up to bed soon after."

"Did you see which way he went in the morning?" asked Oswyl.

"No, sir, sorry. Mornings are a busy time, getting everyone out. He went off afoot, though. No horse for him. That's why I thought, poor scholar, despite the kin-rich mouth."

Penric blinked. "You have a good ear for accents."

"Well, sir, we get a lot of travelers through, at least come summer, and they do tell their tales. Gives a man practice."

Oswyl sat back, frowning, although not at anyone here. "How many nights ago was this, again? Try to be sure."

The tapster, brows crooked with concentration, counted up on his thick fingers. "Six nights, sir. I remember because it was the evening of the horse-market day, and we had a lot of folks in from the country round for that."

Oswyl gave a grunt of satisfaction, drained his tankard, and rose. "Thank you. The Father of Winter's blessing upon this house, in His season impending."

"Go with the gods, sirs."

Learned divine though he now was, Penric did not add the Bastard's blessing, first because most people didn't appreciate the ambiguity, and second because he was incognito for the evening's scouting. And, third, ever since he had once met the god immanent—as close as his arm's reach but not, surely, anything to dare touch—he wasn't exactly comfortable pledging His word. It might not prove to be a safely hollow courtesy.

The Daughter's guard paced before them with a lantern as they made their way back along the dark streets to the Order's house. Penric ventured, "It sounds as if a foray up the valley of the Chillbeck might be worth the time."

Oswyl snorted. "Have you looked at a map? That valley has no good pass out of it to the north. And there are a dozen more just like it. It would be like plunging into a gigantic stone maze."

"It's not so different from my home country, just a hundred miles east of here."

Oswyl eyed him dubiously. "There will be more people on the main road."

"Strangers stand out more in the vales. People notice them. And besides, if that tapster spoke true, you've made up a few days on Inglis's lead since the Crow."

"Time I do not care to waste by haring off up blind alleys."

"Unless the blind alley turns out to be a hunter's bag."

"Hm." Oswyl paused and stared to the north where the high peaks glimmered in the night, a pale wall across the world. "I believe I was right to hold to my reasoning back on the Crow Road. I'd wager that stout Easthome sorcerer is saddle-sore and empty-handed now, somewhere in Saone." The vision seemed to give him a certain understandable satisfaction. "Why should I think your advice better?"

Oddly, Penric didn't sense that the question was rhetorical. "Because this is my home country, not his? Because why would Inglis, if the man was Inglis, ask all those questions and not pursue the pointers they gained him? Because Inglis, being a stranger here, will try the most easily reached routes first?"

"Time," said Oswyl, though his teeth.

"Is it so desperate? He is no less or more trapped by the snow on the passes than he would be by Chillbeck Vale. It's not as though he's been leaving a trail of bodies."

Oswyl was surprised into a noise that came as close to a laugh, if a black one, as Penric had yet heard from him. "I suppose I should not wish it."

An oil lantern hung over the Order's gates, its yellow light glittering from the snow sifted in between the street's cobbles. Oswyl motioned Baar ahead of them into the warm, with a clap to his shoulder and a low-voiced, "Well done, man." But he did not at once follow, and Penric paused with him.

"As a Temple sensitive, have you ever gone out, or been taken out, to check accusations of hedge sorcery?" Oswyl asked abruptly.

Penric, curious at this sudden turn in the talk, folded his arms against the night chill and replied, "Three times, when I was at seminary at Rosehall, I was taken along for training. Not for the working of the thing, since any sorcerer recognizes another as readily as I can tell you are a tall man, but to get a grasp on the legalities, which can become complex. For one thing, just because the accused is not a sorcerer, and they almost never are, it doesn't necessarily mean no crime has been committed, by other means or persons. I did think the false accusations, if the accuser knew them false, to be especially heinous."

Oswyl nodded grimly.

"I've not been sent out since I was made court sorcerer, as Tigney has others to call on for such routine duties. But Desdemona, after she became a Temple demon, went with her riders on hundreds of such inquiries, and found a real sorcerer involved, what—"

Twice.

"Only twice."

"As a locator, I've seen the same from the other side," said Oswyl. "In ten years, only a single case sustained, and the poor man, who'd thought he was going mad, flung himself upon the Temple's mercy and found it. But one time…"

He hesitated so long, Penric nearly prodded him with a, *But one time…?* except that Desdemona quietly advised, *Wait.*

Oswyl glowered down the street at nothing, and finally said, "One time, we were laggard on the road. The reasons seemed sufficient—bad weather, a bridge washed out. Howsoever. We arrived at this dismal village out in the country to discover the accused woman had been burned to death by her frenzied neighbors the night before. No sign found that any demon had jumped from her pyre. She was almost certainly innocent, and if we had arrived timely, we could have disposed of the false charges forthwith, and given stern warnings to the slanderers. As it was, we faced the dilemma of trying to charge an *entire village* with murder. It all broke down in a sickening morass, and in the end…well, no justice was done there, in the Father's sight or any other."

While Penric, taken wholly aback, was still trying to come up with something to acknowledge this that didn't sound fatuous, Oswyl yanked open the door and made to step within. But as he did he growled over his shoulder, "So I *do not like* being late."

The door thudded shut like the end of an argument.

After a moment, Penric sighed and reached for the handle. *This isn't going to be so easy, is it?*

The Father's cases seldom are, noted Desdemona. *Else they wouldn't need* Him.

They rode out of Whippoorwill *very early* the next morning.

VI

*T*WENTY-SEVEN.

Inglis controlled his pained panting, and stropped the knife blade carefully over the shallow cut across his right thigh. When it was well-coated, he set it aside and scrambled around in his fur nest to pull up and tie his trouser strings. He'd found the rest of his clothes in a pile near the hearth; his purse had been unsurprisingly missing. Left boot also there, right boot ruined, cut down the shaft. If it had come off, presumably it could come back on... no. He sighed and abandoned them both.

It took three tries to wallow upright. Arrow sat up and watched with interest. As Inglis hobbled bare-foot the short distance across the hut, the dog rose and paced along. Inglis's hand found its ruff, sturdy but not quite high enough for good support. The wooden door, secured only by a rope latch, creaked wide. He leaned on the jamb and looked around.

The morning sun was blindingly bright on the snow, which was turning slushy in some late teasing thaw, and Inglis's eyes watered. Blinking, he found that the hut was nearly at the tree line. Dark firs and pines fell away below; he could see over their tops down into the vale. The flat valley floor narrowed here, the last farms straggling up its crooked, attenuating length. A small village clustered around a timber bridge over the barely-a-river.

A few more crude huts clung to the slope near Inglis's refuge. One was plainly a smokehouse, from the aromatic haze rising through its thatch. A nanny goat with a bell hung from a leather strap around its neck wandered past, ignoring him. From somewhere nearby, he heard women's voices.

He stared down at Arrow, who gazed back, soulfully attentive. It was worth a try... He caressed the dog's head, and said, **"Fetch me a stick."**

The dog made a cheerful noise in its chest, too deep to be a yip, and bounded away. By the time Inglis had retrieved, cleaned, and sheathed his knife, and determined that no more belongings of his were in the hut, Arrow returned to the doorway, dragging a log as long and thick as a fencepost. He dropped it with a thunk at Inglis's feet and looked up proudly, toothy grin gaping, tail swishing back and forth like a cudgel.

Inglis was surprised into a rusty laugh. It felt strange in his throat. "I said a stick, not building timber!" Though it would make fine firewood. He ruffled the dog's head anyway. "Fetch me a **thinner** stick."

Eagerness unimpaired, Arrow bounded away again. He returned in a few minutes towing something more sapling-like. Inglis broke off the side branches and tested it. It would do for now. The snow was almost not unpleasant on his swollen, throbbing right foot. The left was out of luck. He wondered if he could beg some coverings for them. Limping slowly, he followed the sound of the voices.

In a three-sided shelter, its open face turned to the sun, he discovered a team of women at work scraping a stretched hide. One of them was the girl Beris. The other two were older. All stopped scraping to look up and stare at Inglis, although, as the dog momentarily abandoned him to snatch a pale scrap and retreat to chew on it, the one with the gray braid spared a dispassionate, "Arrow, you fool dog. You'll make yourself sick." Arrow's tail thumped unrepentantly.

"You got up," said Beris, bright and a bit wary. "Are you feeling better now?"

Better than what? "A little," Inglis managed, and, belatedly, "Thank you for your aid."

The middle woman said, "You were lucky to be found. Another few days, and we'd all have gone down to the valley, even the boys." She eyed him in curiosity. "Where were you bound?"

He wasn't sure he could explain his confusion of mind to himself, let alone her, nor how many times he'd switched his goal from Carpagamo to Linkbeck and back. He finally settled on, vaguely, "Up the vale, but I took a wrong turn in the dark." He extended his empurpled foot. "I was wondering if I might beg some rags to wrap my feet. My boots are impossible."

She made a grunt and a motion, which her companions seemed to interpret without difficulty, and levered herself up to trudge off. Gingerly, hoping he would be able to stand again without aid, Inglis lowered himself to another sawed-off chunk of tree trunk that they seemed to be using for camp chairs.

Should he try the 'poor scholar collecting stories' ploy again? It had brought him this far. Arrow relieved him of his dilemma by making another raid on the skin scraps; the woman with the gray braid made a desultory *begone, pest* gesture at him, which he eluded.

"That is an extraordinary dog," Inglis began. Did either of them realize how extraordinary? Two different flavors of blank faces regarded him in return. Beris's seemed innocent. The elder woman's might conceal more. Try manners? He attempted a smile at her, and said, "My name is Inglis, by the way."

"So Beris said."

"And you are, Mother...?"

"Laaxa."

Inglis nodded, as though he cared. Her lips quirked, as though she did. "I was told one of the men who helped bring me off the trail had the dog from his uncle, Scuolla. Can you tell me where to find him to speak to?"

Laaxa snorted. "Where to find him, yes. Though I doubt he'll be speaking to you." She pointed up the valley. "He was killed in a landslide not two months back, poor old man."

The blighting of Inglis's last forlorn hope was as crushingly cold as an avalanche. "Oh." He sat in silence for a minute, too taken aback to think. He finally tried, "Was he the man who raised dogs? I was told there was such a fellow in this vale. Or did he have Arrow from someone else?" Yes, there might be one more possibility...

"Oh, aye, it was something of his trade. His partner was supposed to have inherited them, but they were together out hunting for meat to feed the beasts. *His* body they managed to dig out, at least. The dogs were scattered about to whoever would have them, after. So if you've come seeking to buy one, you might still have a chance."

"Did, uh, you know Scuolla well?"

"Only to nod to. He was no kinsman of mine. He kept to himself up the east branch."

He tried Beris: "Was Savo close to his uncle, do you know?"

She shook her head. "Savo's mother's a lot younger than Scuolla. I don't think they had much to do with each other even before she married and moved to her husband's farm."

He wasn't sure how to ask, *Was your neighbor an illicit hedge shaman?* without frightening them into silence. "Was Scuolla gossips with *anybody?*"

Laaxa shrugged. "He drank with Acolyte Gallin, time to time, I think."

Inglis prodded, "Acolyte Gallin?"

"He's our Temple-man, down Linkbeck." Laaxa waved in the general direction of the valley. Indeed, such a small village was unlikely to rate a full-braid learned divine. An acolyte would typically be made to do. "He serves the whole of the Chillbeck upper vale."

"So he would have conducted Scuolla's funeral rites?"

"Gallin buries pretty much everyone, in these parts."

Inglis worded his next question cautiously. "Did you hear any strange rumors about Scuolla's funeral?"

He'd hit something, because both women gave him sharp, closed looks.

"Wasn't there," said Laaxa. "Couldn't say. You'd have to ask Gallin."

Shamans came as linked chains—half shackles, half lifelines. A shaman was needed not only to culture a Great Beast, but to conduct its sacrifice into each new candidate at the commencement of his or her service. At the end of that life of service, a shaman was again needed to cleanse the comrade soul, free it of that earthly link—some said, contamination—to go on to the gods. Among the reasons for the revival of the royal shamans of the Weald, it was said, was to sustain such chains, that no soul might go sundered. Among the reasons for keeping the practices discreet and contained was to limit such risks. At his own investiture, Inglis had accepted the hazards blithely. He was anything but blithe now.

If Scuolla had indeed been a hedge shaman, as Inglis now strongly suspected, whoever had conducted his investiture was probably long dead; with luck, readied for his last journey by Scuolla himself. So who had cleansed Scuolla in turn? And might that unknown person help Inglis in his woe? *Follow the chain.*

In this high country, it was rumored, the old ways were quietly tolerated by the rural Temple hierarchies, so long as their practitioners conceded precedence and authority to the Temple, and quarterday dues. And if the local Temple folk were not too rigidly virtuous. So was this Acolyte Gallin an enemy of the old ways, or one of the quietly tolerant? And if the latter, had he quietly helped his drinking friend's soul along by securing the services of another hedge shaman to perform those last rites? Or at the very least known where and how, and by whom, they were brought off?

In which case, the next link in Inglis's chain must be to find Acolyte Gallin. Unless this new hope should prove yet another illusion, melting away like the others as his hand grasped for it…the despairing thought made him want, not for the first time, to plunge the accursed knife into his own breast, and be done with this struggle. *One more try.*

Although *One foot in front of the other* was perhaps no longer a very useful self-exhortation. Inglis twisted around. The toy-like houses were only a couple of miles away, as a rock might plummet. Getting himself down the mountain in his current battered condition would be a much trickier problem.

The middle-aged woman returned, her arms full of what looked to be sheepskin scraps and sticks. One of the scraps turned out to be a simple sheepskin cap, folded over fleece-inward and sewn up one side in a sort of triangle, which she plunked unceremoniously over Inglis's head. He jerked but did not rise. "Don't let your ears freeze, lad." The absurd-looking object made a startlingly swift difference in his comfort.

Two sheepskin booties, equally simple, for his other extremities followed; she knelt to fit them over his feet as though he had been a toddler. Outer boots of woven withy and rawhide looked crude but proved clever. He suspected they would grip the snow, though he doubted they'd stand up to a long march. Neither would he, just now. He swallowed a yelp as she tied the rawhide strips on the right foot. "Aye, you've done yourself good, there."

The scraping finished, the three women undid the hide from its clamps and folded it over. Beris rose to stow it away—in a wooden sledge, tucked up in the corner of the shelter. That was how they transported their high-country produce down to the valley, Inglis supposed. Curing a sledge-load of such hides would keep a village worker busy all winter. Could it also transport a half-crippled man?

They couldn't want him to linger here, eating their reserves. It was late for losing him in a crevice. Foisting him on the charity of the village temple must surely seem a better plan.

Inglis wriggled his feet in his sheepskin slippers. "I would pay you, ladies, but I'm afraid someone took my purse."

Beris looked surprised; the middle-aged woman disappointed; Laaxa Graybraid, displeased, but "Hm," was all she said.

"I suspect he still has it, tucked away somewhere." Inglis's memories were too muddled to be sure of identifying the cutpurse by his voice alone, and anyway, whichever of his three rescuers had pocketed it, they had all watched him do so. But there was no way for the thief to spend coins up here, apart from losing them to his friends at dice. "There wasn't much left in it, but enough, I think, to pay for a ride down to Linkbeck." He lifted his hand to indicate the sledge. "With no questions asked." *And none answered.*

A little silence, while they all took this in.

Laaxa vented a pained sigh. "Those boys. I'll see what I can do."

"Thank you, Mother Laaxa."

Arrow, who had stealthily acquired a belly full of hide scrapings, now proceeded to divert his watchers by vomiting them back up again, in a loud and rhythmic paroxysm.

"Eew," said Beris.

"Dogs," sighed the middle-aged woman.

"You going to take that dog?" Laaxa asked Inglis, with a twitch of her gray eyebrows.

"I expect…that will be up to the dog," Inglis replied carefully.

They stared at Arrow, now sniffing his production with evident fascination. Beris hurried to shoo him off, and toss dirt and snow over the slimy pile before he could eat it again.

"Aye," said Laaxa, biting her lip. "I expect so."

VII

*T*HE DAY'S RIDE was slowed by several stops at likely places to inquire after their quarry, all frustratingly fruitless. But it brought Oswyl's troop at length to the village where the local road split off to the valley of the Chillbeck. At the inn there, at last, Oswyl found report of a silent, dark-haired stranger who had spent the night and headed off into the hills, not four days ago. But also of a couple of parties making one final try for the main road north, and one whose destination was the last town within the hinterland's borders.

After a brief debate with the sergeant and the sorcerer, Oswyl made the decision to send two men up the main road tomorrow with strict instructions, if they found the fugitive, not to approach the dangerous man, but to set one guard to follow him and the other to double back and collect their forces. It wasn't a compromise that delighted him in any way, but no one could sensibly go farther this afternoon, with darkness impending and the horses due a rest. Oswyl gritted his teeth in endurance, and made plans to use the evening inquiring of everyone there on the nature of the country roundabout.

A little later, he tracked his sorcerer out to the field behind the inn, where the man had taken it into his strange head to seize the last light and indulge in a stint of archery. It was not a skill in which town-bred Oswyl had much experience, and he watched with reluctant respect as Penric put a dozen arrows into a distant straw bundle, then sent the inn's pot-boy off to collect them.

"Out of practice." Penric frowned at the straw man, at this range now resembling a pincushion, and shook out his bare hands in turn.

"They all hit," observed Oswyl.

Penric rolled his eyes. "Of course they did. The target is *standing still*. If this is to turn into a hunting party in the hills, I need to do better."

"Have you hunted much?"

"In my youth." He delivered this as if his youth had been a half-century ago.

The potboy returned with the arrows, and Penric inquired of Oswyl, lifting his weapon in tentative invitation, "How are you with a bow?"

Not good enough to make a fool of himself in front of this fellow. "I've not had much chance to handle one."

"What, did your father never take you out hunting?"

"My father is an Easthome lawyer. He never passes the city gates if he can help it." Oswyl offered instead, in pointless defense, "I have some training with the short sword."

"Huh." Penric looked nonplussed, as if the very concept of a father who did not dash around in the woods slaughtering animals personally was a novelty. "We didn't hunt for sport, mind you. We needed the game for our table."

Oswyl allowed himself a trace of amusement. "Poaching?"

"Er, no, they were all our lands. My father was Baron kin Jurald. My eldest brother is, now."

"Oh." That was a surprise. It was wrong, of course, to assume that every person of the Bastard's

Order was a bastard or an orphan, or some other odd thing. But it was true often enough. Though this Penric might be one of those acknowledged by-blows with which lords littered the world. Hesitant to pursue that rude curiosity, Oswyl substituted, "How came a kin honorific to be attached to a Darthacan name?" The sorcerer's light coloration made him look entirely a creature of this craggy country.

Penric shrugged. "Some last kin land-heiress met a younger son with few prospects back home in Saone, some generations ago. His dowry didn't last, but the name and the land did." He broke off to send the dozen retrieved arrows flying back into the distant target.

Oswyl wondered if this connection with the minor nobility would give the sorcerer added insight into their outlaw. As the countryside deepened, the palace clerk seemed to be dropping away, to be replaced by...what? Did Penric consider himself a kin warrior, or at least half a one?

Penric might have been entertaining some similar speculation, for as the potboy trotted off again, he asked, "How much of a countryman is our murderer, do you know? Or was he also one of those men who doesn't pass the city gates?" He narrowed his gaze at the peaks that were catching and reflecting the last high light, looming much larger and closer now than back at Martensbridge.

A reasonable question. The great kin lords had town mansions, as well as distant lands like little realms. Increasingly, they also kept more convenient country estates around the capital, such as the kin Boarford manor where all this disaster had started. "I believe he grew up somewhere on the south slopes of the Raven Range, though he's been living with kinsmen in Easthome in late years."

"Hm. I was rather hoping for a city mouse, out of his reckoning in the hills. No such luck for us. A city wolf? Seems a bit contradictory." He glanced at Oswyl. "Or maybe not."

Oswyl had no idea how to respond to that. "Have you ever hunted wolves?"

"A few times, when they came down out of the hills in a starving season."

"Winters like this?"

"Oddly, not so much. Winter is a bad time for the grazers and browsers, weakening them, but for that very reason an easier one for the fanglings that hunt them."

"Did you get them? Your wolves?"

"Oh, yes. We made rugs of the skins."

Penric changed his stance, kneeling, moving, turning, as he sent the next flight of arrows on its way. One missed, and he muttered an oath. "I'd have won a cuff on my ear for that one."

"Your father's love?" Oswyl asked dryly.

"Eh, or Old Fehn, his huntsman. Who'd trained Father. They were pleased to take turns on my ears. Both very keen on taking down the quarry with a first killing shot, if possible. I thought at first it was pious mercy to the Son of Autumn's beasts, but eventually figured out no one wanted to chase all over after a wounded one. Not even me, after I'd tried it a few times."

The foot-weary potboy trudged back, handing over the arrows with a poorly concealed sigh. Penric took his stance and raised his bow once more.

The straw target burst into flames.

The potboy gave a startled yelp. Oswyl jerked back.

Penric merely looked miffed. "Oh, for—! Des, we don't set game *on fire!*" He lowered his bow and glowered at the licking orange flicker, merrily glowing in the gloaming.

"What was that?" Oswyl kept his voice level and didn't let it come out a squeal, barely.

"Desdemona thinks my hunting skills are inefficient. Also, she is bored and wants to go in." He sighed and returned his unloosed arrow to its quiver. His mouth opened and vented a voiceless laugh. He added, peevishly, "I don't know how Ruchia put up with you, really, I don't."

Penric pulled his purse off his belt, dug into it, and handed over a coin to the potboy, now quivering like a restless pony. "Practice over. Off you go." The boy absconded the instant his fingers closed over his payment, looking worriedly back over his shoulder a couple of times in his hasty retreat to the inn yard.

Oswyl wondered to what god he should be praying for luck in *his* chase. Not that any god had ever answered his pleas, whether on his knees by his bed as a boy, or prone in the Temple as a man. He stared glumly at the sorcerer's braided blond queue, pale in the growing shadows, as the man unstrung his bow and reordered his gear, then followed him back inside.

THE VILLAGE of Linkbeck lay high up its vale, past what seemed to Oswyl's Wealdean eye impoverished farms, tending to rocky, tilted pastures rather than grain fields. The cows were fat enough, though, the barns big and solid in fieldstone and dark-stained timber, the houses in a like style, with pale stones scattered over their wood-shingled roofs. The excessively tall mountains loured over all, winter white at their tops, while the valley road was still sodden with autumn mud beneath a crunching, frozen crust. The aspiring river ran green and foaming beneath the wooden span that gave the settlement its name.

The sorcerer pushed his horse up beside Oswyl's as they approached the outskirts, if the half-dozen houses on this side of the river could be so grandly dubbed. "So what is your plan?" Penric inquired—diplomatically, since coming this way at all had been *his* plan.

Oswyl shrugged. "Start with the local Temple divine. Such shepherds tend to be most knowing of the folk about, and will have what news there is." In this backwater, not much, Oswyl suspected, but Penric was right that strangers would stand out; a few villagers working around their places turned to stare as the party rode past. The guard sergeant cast polite, reassuring salutes at them.

Penric cleared his throat. "It might be best not to mention my calling, at first. Or my rank. The former tends to make me a distracting novelty in places like this, rather like a performing bear, and the latter would get either daunted deference from rural Temple folk, or elicit every complaint they have of their superiors who neglect them. As if they could draft me as their messenger."

And neither would speed Oswyl's inquiries. "What should I name you, then?"

Penric tilted his head. "Your assistant, I suppose. Your local guide. Not untrue."

It seemed a curious reticence, from a young man who had seemed proud enough of his rank back in the princess-archdivine's palace. Better, Oswyl supposed, than the off-balance swagger one sometimes observed in those newly promoted to tasks above their weight. They clopped over the bridge and turned onto the main street, where they soon found the local temple. It was built in a style not unlike the barns and houses, fieldstone and dark timber, if taller and six-sided. A little crowd was gathered under a broad portico running the full length of the front, and Oswyl stopped his horse short, flinging up a hand to halt his party. After another moment, Oswyl dismounted to wait more respectfully. Penric followed his lead, coming to stand beside him and watch.

A funeral was in progress, and had reached its most delicate stage, the signing of the gods, or god. Upon a bier decorated with evergreen boughs, a shrouded figure lay. At the head stood a middle-aged man in the five-colored robes of a divine—no, an acolyte, by the single braid looping at his left shoulder. At his sign, what was plainly the family of the deceased shuffled back out of the way to stand attentively along the wall, and the holy animals and their grooms waiting at the side came alert.

A young man had a pet raven perched upon his shoulder, clearly intended as the representative of the Father. A youth, surely a close relative, held a copper-red dog on a leash, its long fur brushed to a silky shimmer, as plainly the emblem of the Son. A leggy girl gripped the lead of a fat white pony, its shaggy hide curried as well as it could be at this season, looking quite appropriate as a beast of the Bastard. An older woman cradled a placid mama cat, marked only by the green ribbon signifying the

Mother around its neck, and a younger girl clutched a squirming kitten, objecting to a like ribbon in blue for the Daughter.

One by one, the acolyte motioned the handlers to the bier. The raven, held out hopefully on the young man's arm, evinced no interest in the proceedings, and hopped back to its shoulder perch. The kitten continued its war with its ribbon. The pony sniffed briefly, causing the people lined up against the wall to stiffen in dismay, but then pulled away, tugging to get its head down and crop some weeds growing up at the corner of the portico. The red dog also sniffed, waving its tail genially but without any obvious excitement. The mama cat jumped down from the woman's arms and curled up neatly upon the chest of the deceased—an elderly grandmother, apparently— and blinked placid gold eyes. A general ripple of relief ran through the mourners, briefly stayed when the dog pulled back, but it was evidently attracted by the cat, not the dead woman, and was swiftly discouraged by a possessive hiss and a swipe of claws.

In great city temples like the ones at Easthome, the signing of which god had taken up the soul of the dead had economic as well as theological significance, as Orders devoted to individual gods took possession of the family's monetary offerings for prayers for the dead. Here, there was likely only one altar table, the colors of its coverings changed out seasonally. It was perhaps shrewd showmanship that had inspired the acolyte to offer the Mother's beast last, rather than cutting things short by beginning with the obvious. Poor these people might be, but not, therefore, paltry.

"That red dog..." muttered Penric out of the corner of his mouth to Oswyl.

"What about it?"

"I think we've come to the right place."

"How so?"

But the sorcerer only made a *wait* wave of his hand, vexingly, although he continued to look around with keen interest.

The acolyte intoned a short prayer, and signed the tally of the gods. The half-dozen burliest men of the family took up the bier and bore it off up the street, and the grooms collected their animals and headed in the opposite direction, quickly losing their formal demeanor. The acolyte, making to follow the bier, glanced uncertainly at Oswyl's party and paused. The woman who had repossessed the mama cat came to his side.

"May I help you, sirs?" he said.

"My name is Locator Oswyl, and I am on a mission of inquiry from Easthome," Oswyl began. As the man jerked his head back in alarm, Oswyl quickly added, "I want to ask after any strangers you may have lately heard about in your district, but we can wait till your duties are done, Acolyte, ah...?"

"Gallin," said the acolyte, looking less alarmed but more curious. "Uh, perhaps my wife, Gossa, can take you in and make you comfortable till I return?"

It wasn't clear which of them he was asking, but the woman, looking equally curious, relieved the cat of its ribbon and set it down, shooing it away with her foot. She bobbed a curtsey at the unexpected visitors. "Indeed, sirs. Follow me."

The children with the animals also paused to stare. Penric cast a special smile at the girl with the white pony, touching his thumb to his lips in a blessing of the white god; the girl looked surprised at this courtesy. Gossa directed what were ever-more-obviously her offspring in assorted directions, the girl with the kitten to stop playing and run ahead to put the kettle on.

The guardsmen with all their horses were sent in the wake of the girl with the pony. Oswyl stepped aside to instruct them, once they had settled the beasts in the temple's stable around back, to spread out through the village and make inquiries as they had done at every stop so far, then hurried to catch up with his reticent sorcerer and the acolyte's wife. Such Temple spouses were often as much the servants of the gods as their mates, if through their mates. She must be a source of local news as good as Gallin.

The acolyte's house was next to the temple, and had little to distinguish it from others along the village street, although the front windows were set with glass, not parchment. It held a cramped but cheerful air suggesting more children than money. The kitchen was set to the back with a sort of parlor-study in front, doubtless where the acolyte performed his spiritual counseling, and to which the visitors were conducted. Oswyl had thus to wait till his hoped-for informant returned from her domestic domain to begin his inquiries. The young girl approached the smiling Penric to show off her kitten, which the sorcerer duly held in his lap and admired. Stroked by his long fingers, it purred like a cogwheel. Oswyl trusted no one else noticed the faint patter of dead fleas drifting off the beast when it was handed back. Oswyl attempted a smile as well, but it apparently lacked the blond man's magic; he was offered no kitten.

Goodwife Gossa, assisted by her dekittened daughter, bustled back in to offer ale, tea, and bread and butter. Penric politely made the sign of the tally before they partook, by way of blessing, which won a smile from Gossa this time. Oswyl's hopes that she might also offer information were quickly dashed, however. At his now-well-practiced queries, she shook her head in regret. No strangers that she'd heard of had arrived in the vale in the past week, or month for that matter. Oswyl cast Penric a reproaching glance.

Penric, undaunted, said to Gossa, "That red dog of your son's. Where did he come by it?"

"Ah, he's a pretty beast, isn't he? But it's a sad tale. The old fellow who raised him was killed in a rock fall not two months back. Some of his dogs had to be dragged away from the place—after days—they mourned him so hard. It was impossible to dig him up to bury him again, so my husband held his rites on the spot. But..." She hesitated, then was interrupted when Gallin came in.

He shrugged off his five-colored robe, which at this range Oswyl could see was a bit threadbare, hung it on a wall peg, and sat to take hot tea with weary gratitude.

"These gentlemen are looking for strangers come to the vale," she informed him, "but I've not heard of any. Have you?"

The familiar, frustrating headshake. "Not too many ever come up this far. We mostly take our own goods to the market at Whippoorwill. A few men from there come up in the summer to trade in animals or hides or cheese, but they aren't strangers."

"I was just starting to tell them about old Scuolla," his wife put in.

Gallin straightened, setting down his mug. He asked more eagerly, "Did someone finally get my letters? Or read my letters? I'd sent to my superiors in Whippoorwill twice, but have got no reply yet. And written to the divines in neighbor vales. One said he could not help, and the other...was less helpful." Gallin grimaced. "My prayers have fared no better."

"Help with what?" asked Oswyl.

"My ghost problem," said Gallin simply.

Oswyl sat back; Penric sat up. "Ghost problem?" he encouraged their host.

Oswyl was not without curiosity, but this side-issue seemed nothing to do with his ever-more-delayed pursuit. His new hope was to extract his party from this local hospitality and get back to the main road by nightfall. Yet Acolyte Gallin seized the opening like a swimmer grasping a rope.

"That luckless old man. I wasn't sure at first, mind you, even with the behavior of his dogs. Not all of them, just his two favorites—Arrow, a fine big fellow, and Blood, that you saw. After the rockslide it seems Arrow had run to the nearest farmyard and barked his head off, till they drove him away by pelting him with stones. Blood stood guard, I suppose you could say, back at the slide, barking and howling. Then that big dog ran all the way into town and found *me*, and whined and carried on and wouldn't be hushed. As the beast seldom left Scuolla's side, it didn't take a Cedonian sage to figure out something was badly amiss. I saddled my horse and followed him up the road, and then the hunting trail, and then, well. Big slide. Took down a lot of trees. I'd heard the crash echoing down the vale earlier that morning, but when no alarm had come, I'd dismissed it. It didn't take me long to find the remains of Scuolla's apprentice, and one of the other dogs, its back broken, sadly, but it had been too late for either of them from the first. A gang of men from the village, later that afternoon, had no better luck at finding Scuolla, though we did uncover one more dog, and buried both beasts properly, no skinning. I did insist on that, for respect." He nodded to himself. Neglected by his Temple supervisors in this remote vale, Gallin had perhaps taken to self-supplying their absent discipline or praise. Oswyl tried not to sympathize.

After a long, thoughtful, silent inhalation through his nose, Penric came out with, "And how long had you known that old Scuolla was a hedge shaman?"

Intent on recapturing the conversation by offering suitable condolences and then hurrying their leave, Oswyl swallowed his words so fast he coughed. *What?*

Gallin cast the young man a closer look than heretofore. "I've served in this vale for over twenty years. I found out what he was early on, but not so early that I hadn't had time to learn his kin and his ties, and that there was no harm in him. I take my first duty to be to souls, not laws. And to learn as well as teach, or what else do the gods put us in this world for?"

"Indeed." Penric made the tally sign; coming from a full-braid Temple divine (even one who'd left his braids in his saddlebags), it seemed to Oswyl strangely more than a mere assenting shrug.

Reassured by this reaction, Gallin went on: "My trust was repaid five-fold, through those years. Scuolla was as pious a man as any and more than many, and he and his dogs were an aid to all in need, lost or hurt, in flood or fire or famine and a hundred smaller tasks. In time, I came to think of him as my good left hand here in the vale, without which the right could not grip half so well."

Gossa, nodding in confirmation to all this, put in, "That's why we don't understand about his funeral." She made a *go on* gesture at her husband.

Penric's eyes narrowed. "It took place at the rockslide, your goodwife said?"

"Aye. There was no getting down to his body. For a time we thought the dogs might find him, or later, our noses, but he was too deep for the last and the dogs, well, the dogs never settled on a consensus. Or settled at all—very disturbed they were, right to the last. In the event, no god signed to taking up his soul, or at least none we could discern, though we made the trial five times, till the holy animals began to bite and scratch and kick and it grew dark."

"Could he have escaped the fall somehow?" asked Oswyl, ensnared by this tale despite himself.

"Run off for some reason?" The dead companion was suggestive, to a suspicious mind.

Gallin huffed out a breath. "I wondered about that, too, as things went on. But it doesn't stand up to the witness of the dogs."

In his past investigations, Oswyl had found many mute things to give testimony that shouted; he supposed he must now add dogs to that list. At least his superiors could not chide him for not swearing them in. "Sundered, then."

Gossa made a fending gesture in front of her bodice, and scowled at him as fiercely as one of his aunts about to correct his legal rhetoric.

Gallin shook his head and went on, "By every sign, Scuolla was sundered, and I don't think he should have been. I *know* he would not refuse the gods. And if the Son of Autumn, to Whom he'd made devotions all his life, didn't think him good enough somehow, well, there's still the Bastard. So where was *He?* Where were any of Them?"

An unanswerable question that Oswyl had confronted many times in his career. He bit his lip.

"The thing is," put in Gossa, "everyone round about now takes that rockslide for haunted, and avoids it."

Penric laced and unlaced his fingers a few times, then seemed to come to some decision. "So this hedge shaman, working with dogs as the medium of his art, died uncleansed of the Great Beast that must have given him his powers. And now his soul is lost between the worlds, a sundering unwilled by either the gods or the man."

"You know so much of such things, young fellow?" said Gallin, startled.

"I'm, ah…something of a Temple sensitive myself, as it happens." His smile had gone a little stiff. "I knew the moment I saw the red dog that there had to be a shaman in this tale somewhere. It is partway to being made a Great Beast, did you know?"

Gallin cleared his throat. "Blood's a very intelligent dog. Well-mannered. Good with all the village children. Took to being a holy animal with no trouble at all."

"I daresay."

"So…you didn't come here in answer to my letters…?" The acolyte seemed reluctant to give up this hope.

"Not to your letters, no." Penric bared his teeth in a brief, ironic grimace, an edged look Oswyl had not seen in his face before.

Gallin confessed, "I'd thought to find another hedge shaman for Scuolla, somewhere up or down the mountains, to perform their last secret rites for him. Him seeming out of reach of my prayers. Scuolla had his Great Beast from the shaman here before him, long ago when he was a young man, and performed the cleansing for his mentor in turn when he died. He was bringing along his own apprentice, but he'd not invested the man with his powers yet as far as I know. Well, I do know, for Wen's soul was signed taken up by the Son at his funeral the day after the tragedy."

Gossa nodded. "Plain as plain, that one was. Greatly to his family's relief amidst their grief."

Oswyl began, "I should explain something more about the fugitive we hunt—" but Penric flung up his hand, interrupting him.

"Wait just a little on that, Locator, if you please."

It didn't please Oswyl much, but Penric was turning to Gallin. "How far is it to this maybe-haunted rockslide of yours?"

"About five miles up the East Branch road, or thereabouts. An hour's brisk ride." Gallin squinted intently at Penric. "You say you are a Temple sensitive. Can you sense ghosts?"

"Ah…with a bit of special help, yes."

"Can you get that help?"

"I carry it with me."

Gallin grew eager. "Could you—would you—would you be willing to ride out to the fall with me, and sense what you can? It would put my mind to rest." He reflected. "Or not, but at least I'd *know*."

Such an expedition couldn't be back till nightfall, Oswyl calculated. They would be stuck in this village till tomorrow. *"Time,"* he gritted under his breath.

Penric's glance flicked up. He murmured back, "You could go on without me."

"No. I can't."

"Well, then." He turned to the acolyte. "I'm willing to take a look, yes. I can't make any promises."

Gallin actually clapped his hands in relief. "We can be off as soon as the horses are saddled."

"We should take the red dog," added Penric.

Gallin stilled. "Ah. Aye." He rose to lead the way, pausing only to grasp his wife's hands in a farewell. At least the goodwife eyed them all more approvingly, as they clumped out after him.

VIII

---

*P*ENRIC STUDIED THE dog, Blood, as it cantered along behind the acolyte's horse. It wasn't undog, or not-dog, or even, really, terribly uncanny. It was just...more-dog, a peculiar density of itself.

Can you show me more? he asked Desdemona.

You are seeing what I am seeing, more or less, she replied. *Turnabout being fair play.*

Hm.

Oswyl nudged his horse up beside Pen's on the rutted wagon trail—it was unduly flattering to dub it a road. After a moment he murmured, "You really can sense ghosts?"

"Desdemona can. I don't have her share the sight with me unless I ask. It's distracting, especially in old places where many people have died over the years." When first this skill had come to him, a few months after Des had moved in, he'd tripped himself up dodging around things no one else could see, much to her amusement, till he'd worked out how to get her to shut it off. Some people had thought he'd been taken with fits. The real explanation hadn't improved things by much.

"Can all sorcerers do so?"

"I imagine it varies. Those possessing younger or less experienced demons may be less adept."

"I wonder that my Order does not requisition them more. The ability to interrogate the dead… would be most helpful in the instance of a murder."

"Mm, not as much as you'd think. Most souls go at once to their gods, when severed from their bodies. It's the god who is present at the funeral, not the person. An invoked messenger." An odd thing when Pen thought about it, that so great a Presence should stoop to so small a task.

Oswyl frowned in what Pen was beginning to recognize as professional frustration. As distinguished from the dozen other ways he could frown.

"In any case," Pen consoled him, "it would be hard for the sensitives to correctly interpret and report what they see. Even a fresh ghost still holding the form of its body can't speak. The sundered soon grow muddled, like an old man who's lost his wits along with his teeth. They exhaust the ability to assent to their god by the time they exhaust their ability to refuse. Which is what makes them sundered, I suppose." Indifferent, beyond attachment or pain, attenuating into pale smudges, and then, at length, gone. Pen wasn't sure he could convey how disturbing this process was to see, midway, without being frightening, exactly. Well, not after the first brush.

You squeaked in terror, said Des.

Did not, Pen thought back. *That was just a yelp of surprise.* The ghosts, once understood, had seemed less horrifying than his first fear, that he was hallucinating or going mad. Still, not *comfortable.*

Gallin turned his horse aside onto a narrower trail, weaving up through the trees, and Pen and Oswyl fell into single file behind him. After a damp, scrambling time, Blood bounded ahead, whining, and the steep woods opened out abruptly onto the rock fall.

Rock fall was a serious understatement, Pen realized. The slide was perhaps a hundred paces across and three times that in height, a fan of debris including boulders the size of wagons, mud, and a tangle of uprooted and snapped trees. At its wide foot, the local stream had backed up and routed around; at its narrower head, a raw and ragged new cliff marked where it had heaved itself out of the mountain's weakened side. He imagined being caught under the roar, not knowing whether to run forward or back, so screened by the trees on the shuddering path as not to know either was equally futile till too late.

The three horsemen all pulled up at the edge, but Blood sprang onward, scrambling over the treacherous footing, sniffing and uttering small yips. Penric did not at first see what the dog sought, and then, at a shift from Desdemona, did.

Oh.

The old man sat on a boulder midway across the scree and a little down from where the path was cut off. He wore the common garb of workmen in this country, boots, trousers, rough-spun shirt, a capacious sheepskin vest fleece turned inward and hanging open around him. A short-brimmed hat was pushed back on his head, a few feathers stuck in its band. Penric could not discern their hues, for feathers, clothes, and the man who wore them were all faded to a colorless translucency.

As Pen watched, Blood made his way, not quite unerringly, to the man's side, and whimpered and yipped around him like a dog sniffing around a badger's den that was too small to enter. The man smiled faintly and lifted his hand to stroke the dog's head. The beast calmed and sat, silky tail waving like a signal flag.

Pen dismounted and handed his reins to Oswyl. "Hold my horse, please."

"Can you see anything?" asked Gallin anxiously.

"Oh, yes." Pen turned and began to clamber across the debris.

"Be careful!" called Gallin. "It could be unstable!"

Pen waved understanding.

Incurious as an old idler on a town square bench, the man watched him approach. Pen's gloves saved him from tearing his hands as he tested each hold, seeking balance rather than suspect support. He was breathing heavily by the time he arrived at the boulder and found firm-ish footing. He stared down at the revenant, who stared back up but then returned his attention to his worried dog

"Master Scuolla," Pen tried. "Shaman, sir."

The man seemed not to hear. But he had noticed Pen, and was most certainly interacting with the dog. A sundered soul some, what, two months into its dissolution ought to be a lot more vague than this. More distanced.

He looks as if he hasn't been dead more than a few days, Des agreed.

Have you seen anything like this before?

Des shook Penric's head. *The only shaman I ever met was very much still alive.*

Can you reach him any more directly?

No more than we have done.

Feeling rude, Pen tried passing his hand through the man's head. Any chill was indistinguishable from the mountain air. The man lifted his face as if to a passing breeze, but then returned his attention to his dog, who fawned on him.

Des had gone quiet. Pen stood back and thought. His thoughts were extremely uncomfortable. The most uncomfortable of them was that this called as much for the skills of a divine as a sorcerer. He made the five-fold tally, and tried to compose his mind in prayer. Asking his god, or indeed any of the gods, for a sign seemed a madly dangerous thing to do, but in any case no sign was forthcoming. In the silence, he stared across the scree at Acolyte Gallin, and contemplated the disquieting notion that maybe he wasn't supposed to be the supplicant, here. Maybe he was supposed to be the *answer*.

But old Scuolla needs a shaman, not a sorcerer. And while Locator Oswyl had been trying to lay hands on his fugitive shaman for weeks, so far they'd come up empty.

Well, if the dead man had lingered here for two months, he probably wasn't going anywhere else immediately. Though time was clearly not his friend. Pen called to Blood, who ignored him, and made his way, slipping and sliding, back across the rock fall to the horses.

"Could you sense anything?" asked Acolyte Gallin.

"Oh, yes. He's there, all right. Communing with his dog, although not much with me."

Oswyl blinked at him, startled, and stared across at Blood licking the air by what must appear to him a bare boulder. Licking at Scuolla's ghostly hand, his tongue sliding through it in chill confusion.

Gallin signed himself, looking distraught. "He is sundered, then."

"Ah…" said Pen. "Maybe not yet."

"Surely it is too late…?"

"I can't claim to know what's going on here. My first guess is that his shamanic powers allow his spirit to still draw some nourishment from the world even though separated from his body. But it's been a long time. He seemed…it's hard to explain… tired. I think he's still fading, but more slowly than other men would."

"Then there's still a chance to save him? If a shaman might be found?"

"If a shaman might be found, it would still be worth a try, at least."

Gallin's breath huffed out, as he stared across to where Blood lingered by the side of his old comrade and friend. "If there are any such powers hiding elsewhere in these mountains, my letters should have brought me *some* word by now."

Not your letters. Your prayers. And Penric wasn't going to say *that* out loud.

Oswyl was acquiring a whole new frown, as he perhaps made some of the connections Pen just had. Or at least noticed the excessive amount of coincidence starting to pile up. As a locator, he was surely suspicious of coincidences. As a divine,

Penric was too, but in a very different way. He remembered the shrewd gray eyes of the Saint of Idau, and the white god who had once looked through them at him. *At us.* Desdemona, remembering with him, shuddered.

"In any case, we can do nothing more here right now." Pen retrieved his reins from Oswyl and swung himself back up into his saddle.

Gallin called Blood, who didn't come until Scuolla's ghost made a releasing sort of *go on* gesture. The acolyte then offered the hospitality of the Linkbeck Temple to Oswyl's party for the night—Linkbeck lacked an inn as such, although Gallin assured them he could find beds for all among his villagers, no need to camp in the stable loft. He looked back over his shoulder as they turned onto the path again, and breathed in a hesitant undertone, "Not hopeless?"

Penric wasn't sure to whom that was addressed, but answered, "I am not certain. Locator, perhaps the time has come to explain the full story of the man we seek."

Oswyl gestured assent, but did not begin till they turned back onto the wagon track and he could ride side-by-side with Gallin. Penric fell behind, listening. Gallin made exclamations at all the expected high and low points, till Oswyl, drawing toward the end of his account, let fall a *Learned Penric*.

Gallin turned in his saddle and stared in astonishment. Penric returned a wary smile and a little wave of his fingers. He was unsurprised when Oswyl finished and Gallin dropped back beside him, brows crooked in new inquiry. It was embarrassing when a man twice his age looked to *him* for answers, especially when he didn't have them.

"You are really a sorcerer, and a full-braid divine?"

Pen cleared his throat. "Long story. But all Temple sorcerers must undergo a divine's training and oaths. We seldom take up the duties of a regular divine, though."

Gallin seemed to consider this, sidelong. "Does your Order *have* regular duties?"

Pen puffed a laugh. "Good question. We go where we're needed, I think."

"And yet you were not sent?" Gallin asked as Oswyl reined back to Penric's other side, trapping him in the center of their attention. The acolyte looked across: "Either of you?"

Oswyl shook his head.

Penric said slowly, "I think we may no longer be hunting. We may be trapping. If that innkeeper told us true, Inglis kin Wolfcliff seeks another shaman. Find the nearest one, and he may come to us." Come, be brought or be driven—this game would not evade such Beaters as Penric had begun to suspect were in play.

Gallin said plaintively, "But why should a shaman seek a shaman? What could a royal shaman, even a disgraced one, possibly want with a mere country hedge shaman?"

Another good question. That their quarry sought such a practitioner had been enough to direct their pursuit. Maybe he should have thought a step further…? Des snorted.

Oswyl's logical mind was starting to work on the question. He offered tentatively, "He seeks to take refuge with someone who will hide him?"

Penric threw in, "Or perhaps he plans a suicide, yet does not want to be sundered like poor Scuolla." Yes, suicide must pose a problem for such an invested person. Some suicides sought sundering, but many another was hurrying to the hoped-for refuge of their god. The Temple spent a good deal of effort trying to discourage that particular approach to divinity.

Oswyl chewed this over, looking as though he did not like the taste. "Beyond my mandate," he said at last.

But not beyond mine...in principle. Another disturbing thought. Today seemed unusually full of them.

At the sound of hoofbeats, Penric looked up to see a rider cantering toward them. After a moment, he recognized one of their guardsmen, Heive.

"Sirs!" he called, reining in before them. "Daughter be thanked, I found you. Goodwife Gossa and my sergeant beg that you return at once. A stranger has come to the village, and he could be the man we seek. Dark hair and a Wealdean accent, at least, though oddly dressed, and I couldn't swear to his age."

"You've seen him?" said Oswyl, rising in his stirrups in excitement. "You haven't tried to approach him, have you?"

"No, sir," said Heive fervently. "He came to the acolyte's house, seeking him, he said. Goodwife Gossa told him you were out on an errand and sent him to wait in the temple, and for me to ride for you. The sergeant and Baar are watching the building from a distance. He'd not come out by the time I left."

"We'd best hurry," said Gallin in a voice choked with alarm, and led the way, kicking his horse into a canter. Oswyl was right on his heels. Penric and Heive fell in behind; Blood ran after them. Pen was suddenly glad he'd brought his bow along, rather than leaving it with his saddlebags in the temple stable.

At some risk of bringing in the horses wet and winded, they made fast time back to the village street, finding it bare of villagers. They stopped a few houses away from the temple. The guard sergeant waved from where he hunkered down behind someone's garden gate, and pointed to the temple door. "Still in there," he mouthed.

Oswyl returned a silent salute. They all dismounted. Blood, panting and muddy, made a lunge for the temple doors. Gallin grabbed him by the scruff of his neck and hauled him, whining, to his house, where Gossa could be seen peeking through the front window, beckoning urgently at him. Pen unlaced his bow from his saddle, strung it, and shrugged on his quiver. The other two guardsmen joined them. The armed party made its way quietly to the temple portico.

Oswyl gestured Penric ahead. "All right, sorcerer," he muttered. "Go on."

Wait, what, all by myself? "Wouldn't it be better for us all to rush him at once?"

The expressions on four faces seemed to disagree with him. "If this is a false lead," said Oswyl, "you are the one man among us who can tell at a glance."

Gallin and Gossa came out the door of their house, and stood holding hands and watching Pen anxiously. Pen swallowed, nocked his arrow, and stepped into the dimness of the temple's interior.

Light me, he thought to Desdemona, and the shadows fled from his eyes, leaving his vision clear.

The man lay prone on the wooden temple floor, just this side of the cold fire plinth, arms out, in what would be the attitude of deepest supplication, except he was not aimed toward any wall shrine in particular. Penric wasn't sure if he was seeing prayer, or exhaustion. He was unshaven and wore a grab-bag of garb, townsman's clothing but a peasant's woven-withy boots, and a mountaineer's sheepskin cap. One hand gripped a long stick. By his side lay a huge dog, black and tan, head down on crossed paws in an attitude of canine boredom. Its head came up at Pen's approach, triangular ears pricked; its tail thumped desultorily on the boards, although it also growled. Perhaps both it and Pen were equally confused?

If Blood had been more-dog, this one was even more so, dense with presence. *This is a Great Beast. Not so, Des?*

Impressive, she conceded.

"Sit up," Pen commanded, in what he hoped was a convincing arresting-officer voice; "But don't get up."

The man jerked to his knees, grabbing for his stick to support his stance. His sleeve, falling back, revealed an arm crisscrossed with long, vicious-looking scabs. The knife at his belt glowed with strange power swirling like an aurora, not in Pen's eyes but in Des's. He stared wildly at Pen, mouth falling open as he drew sudden breath. The dog stood up and growled with what seemed a lot more authority than Pen had mustered.

"Inglis kin Wolfcliff," said Pen, certain now of what he faced. And then had no idea of what to say next. This whole scene was so sideways to any of his preconceptions about the man, anything he might have rehearsed would have been worthless anyway. As neither man nor dog launched himself at Pen's throat, he eased the tension on the string and let his bow droop, but still held it ready. "We've been looking for you."

IX

*I*NGLIS USED HIS stick to climb to his full height, although his right leg, much abused by the trip down the mountain this morning, threatened to buckle from the pain. The man before him seemed a blond apparition, inexplicable. **"Go away,"** Inglis tried.

The intruder just tilted his head. "Good attempt, wolf-man. A bit misdirected. Although wouldn't 'Give me your horse' seem more to the point?"

How did he *know...*? And then, however badly his powers were crippled, Inglis recognized the fellow for what he was. And, five gods, or should that oath be *Bastard's teeth!*, he *was*. His spirit-density was stunning. "Sorcerer." Inglis was confounded by hope and fear. And by hurt, and heartache, and exhaustion, and his long, futile flight. "Temple, or hedge?" Or, five gods help them all, rider or ridden? Surely any demon so powerful must be ascendant? Could Inglis persuade it to...

"Temple through and through, I'm afraid. You are not more surprised than I was." He glanced aside at Arrow, who had shifted to stand at Inglis's right hand. "How did you come by one of Scuolla's dogs?"

"It found me. Up on the mountain. When I was lost, trying to find a shortcut to the Carpagamo road. It won't stop following me." Wait, how did he know of Scuolla?

"Ah. Huh." The blond man's lips crooked up in a smile of...dismay? "Did it bring you here, do you think?"

"I...don't know." *Had* it? He glanced down at the big dog, his companion for days. Inglis had assumed the animal was attracted to him because he was a shaman invested, and it had somehow confused him with its prior master. *Maker.* "I came looking for..." He hardly knew what, anymore.

"You came looking for Acolyte Gallin, I understand. Why?"

"An old woman up at the summer grazing camp told me that he knew Scuolla. I thought he might know...something."

"Did you know Scuolla has been dead under a rock fall for the past two months?"

"I was told that, too."

"And did she tell you that he was a hedge shaman?"

"No. I...guessed it. From the dog."

"Hm." The sorcerer seemed to come to some decision. "I have a senior locator outside, who has ridden all the way from Easthome in pursuit of you. Do you surrender? No more shaman tricks, no running away?"

What could this man do if he refused? "I'm not running anywhere." Inglis grimaced. "I mangled my leg on the mountain."

The sorcerer looked him up and down. "Ah. I *see*. Yes, mountains will do that."

Inglis hung on his staff, feeling sick. "They in Easthome seek me as a murderer?"

"Locator Oswyl is a very precise man. I'm sure he'd say he seeks you as a *suspected* murderer. No one is going to hang you on the spot, you know, without all those judicial ceremonies his Order is so fond of. Everyone has to dress up, first. Not to mention what could be some fraught theological complications." He added, "I think you had better give me your knife, for now."

"NO."

He went on with unimpaired weird cheer, "That's Tollin kin Boarford's ghost wrapped in it, yes? So Oswyl was right. I shall like to know, later, how you managed that. Speaking from my calling. Both of them, come to think."

"I'm not going to use it to stab anyone." Inglis's voice was hoarse. "Else."

"Yes, but my colleagues won't know that. Once things are more settled, I may even be able to give it back into your care. You've been faithful so far, haven't you? You've brought it a long way." His voice had gone soft, persuasive. Sensible. "Why?"

"I sought a shaman."

"You are a shaman."

Inglis vented a bitter laugh. "Not anymore."

The blond man looked him over. Or *through* him? "Surely, you are."

"I *tried*. I *can't*. Can't enter the trance." His voice, rising, fell. "I think it is a punishment. Maybe from the gods."

The sorcerer raised his eyebrows. "So why not take your problem to your shamanic superiors at court in Easthome? They were much closer."

"I *killed* Tollin," Inglis said through his teeth. "I could not go back there and face...everyone."

The sorcerer took a quick glance over his shoulder. Yes, there were some other men hovering outside the door. No other exits. *Trapped. How?*

"Oh? I was told he'd been disemboweled by a boar. Did you stab him before, or after?"

"After. It was...it was a mercy cut." Inglis shuddered at the memory of the knife blade going in, the pressure and the give in his hand, all mixed up with his visions as he'd descended from the plane of symbolic action, exhilarated to have completed his first investiture, to have made a fierce spirit warrior in truth. Tollin's agonized face... "He was screaming." *It was unbearable. I had to shut him up.*

"He could not have survived his injuries from the boar?"

"No. Gods, no."

"Why didn't you go for help then?"

"It was...very confusing in that moment. He must have planted his knife in the beast's neck even as he was being ripped open. I captured its spirit and passed it into Tollin before I came back to, back to, to the sty. To the blood." His wolf-within had been wildly excited by the blood, nearly uncontrollable. Inglis could, he supposed, have claimed that he'd lost control of his powers in that moment. He'd considered that defense, on his long ride north. *But I didn't. Not really.*

That came later.

"Came back…out of your shamanic trance?"

"Yes."

"Did you mean to bind his spirit to your knife?"

"No! Yes…I don't know. I don't know how I did that." Well, Inglis knew *what* he'd done. He'd been taught about the banner-carriers, hallowed Old Wealdean warriors who were charged with carrying away from the field of battle the souls of their fallen spirit-warrior comrades. And the souls of those dying but not yet dead. The fatally wounded must have included kinsmen, friends, mentors. Had those mercy cuts, to sever the soul from its body and bind it to the banner for that strange rescue, been as horrible for them as it had been for him? *I think it must.*

"Was this investiture Tollin's idea, or yours?"

"His. He'd badgered me for weeks. But none of this would have happened if I hadn't agreed to try the rite. I wanted to test my powers. And...and then there was Tolla."

"His sister, yes? Oswyl mentioned her. I gather your courtship was not prospering. So why not use your weirding voice on her directly?"

Inglis glared at him, offended. Arrow growled.

"Nah, nah." The sorcerer gave a dissimulating wave of his fingers. "You have a romantic heart, I see." As Inglis glared harder, he went on, "I'm Learned Penric of Martensbridge, by the way. Temple sorcerer of the Bastard's Order, presently serving the court of the princess-archdivine, who assigned me to this Grayjay..." He jerked his head toward the doorway.

That near-youth was a Temple divine? Yes, he had to be, to be entrusted with his demonic passenger. Beyond Learned Penric Inglis saw another man entering the temple hall. Three more clustered behind him, two armed with short swords and one with a cavalry crossbow, and following them, yet another fellow—middle-aged, shabbier, anxious.

"What kept you?" Penric, still not turning, asked of the lead man behind him. Keeping Inglis in his eye. But Penric's sturdy hunting bow was now dangling disregarded from his hand. He slid his arrow back into his quiver.

"I didn't want to interrupt," said the first man. "Your inquiries seemed to be faring well." His accent was pure Easthome. Beneath his cloak, Inglis made out gray fabric, and the glint of brass buttons. *The locator.* The armed three were Temple guardsmen of some sort, Inglis supposed, dressed in a mishmash of local winter woolens and bits of blue uniform.

Penric at last glanced back to the doorway. "And here is Acolyte Gallin, shepherd of this valley," he continued, naming the older fellow, who was gaping at Inglis in inexplicable amazement. "The very man you sought. Now that you have found him, what?"

"I wanted to find what shaman in turn had cleansed Scuolla." Inglis swallowed. "Discover if he could also free Tollin. Cleanse him so he is not sundered. We were both fools together, but Tollin does not deserve *that.*"

Gallin stepped forward, looking pole-axed. "I prayed for a shaman. And here you are, right here—!"

Penric, watching Inglis stare back in bewilderment, put in with a helpful air, "Scuolla has not been cleansed, because no other shaman could be found. But he is not yet sundered. I'm not sure what sustains him. I suspect he may be drawing some spiritual nourishment from his dogs."

Inglis's black yelp was scarcely a laugh. "Then your prayers must have been heard by the Bastard, Acolyte Gallin. To bring you a shaman who *can't work his craft...!*"

The sorcerer-divine pursed his lips, as if seriously considering this jibe. "That just might be so. He *is* the god of murderers and outcasts, among His other gifts." He added under his breath, "And vile humor. And rude songs."

"*I can't cleanse anyone.*" Too polluted himself by his crime...?

"Not in your current state of mind, clearly," said the sorcerer. His tone had grown easy, friendly. Had he understood *any* of this? "I think..."

Everyone in the temple hall seemed to hang on his breath.

"We should all go have dinner. And get a good night's sleep. Yes."

Oswyl and the guardsmen stared at Penric in startled disbelief, as if he'd just proposed they all grow wings and fly to Carpagamo, or something equally bizarre.

"That sounds very sensible." A slight quaver in Acolyte Gallin's voice undercut this endorsement. "The sun is already gone behind the mountains."

"Aren't you going to magic him?" the lead guardsman asked Penric, nodding warily at Inglis. Inglis couldn't tell if that was something he'd wanted to see, or to be far away from.

"I don't think I need to. Do I?" Penric, smiling, held out his hand to Inglis, palm up. Waiting for him to surrender his knife, which would be surrender indeed. "By the way, how are you keeping Tollin from fading?"

For answer, Inglis mutely held up both arms, letting his sleeves fall back.

"Oh," said Penric, quietly.

"Blood holds life even after it leaves the body," said Inglis, his voice falling unwilled into the cadences of his teachers. His own despair added, "For a little while."

"Mm, yes, one sees why your Darthacan ancestors were frightened of the forest magics," murmured Penric. "It's written that the old shamans worked some very strange effects with blood. Rather a different affair if using someone else's blood, and not one's own, I imagine. Theologically speaking." His smile was unwavering.

Inglis's weary will was not. With fumbling fingers, he picked out the rawhide ties securing his sheath to his belt, and handed the knife across. Penric touched forehead, lips, navel, groin, and spread his fingers over his heart, *Daughter-Bastard-Mother-Father-Son*, completing the blessing in full before taking it. Sorcerer he might be, possessed of fearsome powers, but in this moment the full-braid divine was clearly ascendant. He didn't hold it like a weapon. He held it like a sacrament.

He sees.

Lightheaded to the point of passing out with this release from his deathly burden, Inglis fell to his knees, burying his face in the thick fur of Arrow's neck, gasping against tears. The dog whined and tried to lick him.

From outside the temple, a woman's voice cried, "Blood, you fool beast! Come back here this instant!"

A copper-colored dog with muddy paws rushed into the temple hall. Inglis nearly fell over as Arrow jerked away from him. For a moment, he gathered himself to break up a dog fight, but the two animals exchanged greetings with happy yips and whines, circling around to sniff each other's nether parts. Old friends, it seemed.

And another survivor of the rock fall? The red dog was thick with spirit-density, although not nearly so much as Arrow. Halfway to being a Great Beast; doomed to be sacrificed at the end of its life into a new puppy, to continue layering up its powers. Inglis wondered if Scuolla would have made sure it was a long and happy life, by dog standards. The good natures of both beasts suggested so.

The two dogs then turned their attentions to Inglis, swarming around him, nosing and licking and nearly knocking him over again. He was surprised into an almost-laugh fending off Blood leaning up trying to taste his face.

A woman trotted into the hall and halted beside Gallin. Middle-aged, careworn, clearly his helpmate. "He broke out when I opened the door," she wheezed.

Learned Penric, watching the play in amusement as Blood fawned on Inglis, rubbed his lips and murmured, "Take witness of the dogs, Locator?"

Oswyl just looked exasperated. "This benighted case is the strangest I ever worked on. And I'm going to have to *report it all* when I get home, you realize?"

Learned Penric's blue eyes crinkled as he grinned. "You'd best pray for eloquence, then."

X

IN OSWYL'S PRIOR investigations, requisitioning
support from the local Temple usually meant
finding his bed and board at a chapterhouse of one of
the Orders, or a pilgrim hostel attached to the main
center, or at least a recommended inn. Linkbeck did
not boast any of these, nor a jail, nor a secure lockup
in some outbuilding, nor even manacles on the cellar
wall of a crumbling stronghold. His prisoner must
needs remain under the direct supervision of the
sorcerer at all times. This resulted in their having
to impose on the domestic hospitality of Gallin and
Gossa; mostly, as it turned out, Gossa.

Oswyl was deeply uncomfortable with bringing
a maybe-murderer-mage into their home, but the

couple seemed to take it in stride. An extra trestle table to increase the seating by six was swiftly set up by Gallin and his sons. Gossa had apparently handled sudden refugees from disasters in the vale this way many times before, driving her children and the servant girl, whom Oswyl had last seen leading the Bastard's white pony at the funeral, this way and that. It didn't take her long to draft the guardsmen as well, easing Oswyl's conscience slightly. Oddments of food appeared spontaneously, as if in a tale of an enchanted castle, dishes sent over by neighbors to supplement the family's fare.

All the chaos coalesced in a surprisingly short time in seating twelve to dinner, plus the two dogs lurking under the table, whether following Inglis or in hope of scraps. Learned Penric looked discomfited when asked by the acolyte to bless the meal, but he delivered the formula with a seminary-trained grace, which seemed to please their hosts. The soup was hardly watered at all.

Inglis was a blot of silent misery in this active company. Perhaps feeling the contrast, he did exert himself to politeness, belying his unkempt brigand's looks. Someone had taught him table manners, certainly. Oswyl grew aware that Gallin, too, was watching the shaman closely. His dark presence was daunting enough that no one tried to draw him into the table talk, more to Oswyl's relief than otherwise. Perhaps to make up for this, Penric, seated on his other side from Oswyl, contributed an unexceptionable tale or three, especially after the women found out he served at the princess-archdivine's court in what they evidently thought of as exotic, distant, romantic Martensbridge. The sorcerer seemed as much an object of muted wonder as the murderer; Oswyl was not used to his inquirer's menace being so eclipsed.

After a brief post-dinner consultation with Oswyl, Gallin and Gossa sensibly sent the children off to find the beds with the neighbors, and kept Oswyl's party all together in their house. Gossa faltered at a social dilemma: Learned Penric obviously had to be offered the best bedchamber, but Inglis perforce must accompany him there, Oswyl wanted to keep a close eye on both, and the dogs would not be parted from the prisoner. Gossa almost drew the line at the dogs, but Penric charmed her into a reprieve, promising her they would not leave fleas in her beds.

Oswyl pulled Penric aside on the staircase. "Do you think he could control those dogs? They could prove as much a weapon as his knife."

"I suspect the dogs may have their own design. Or someone's design," Penric returned in matching quiet tones. Earlier, he had tied the thongs of the knife sheath around his neck and tucked the knife out of sight in his shirt; he now touched his chest. "And Gossa has bigger knives in her kitchen. This is a hostage, not a weapon."

"Do you think Inglis may attempt escape? He claims to have lost his shamanic powers, but he could be lying."

"Or mistaken," murmured Penric. "Or have mislaid them. I'm rather counting on mislaid, but we'll have to see. Anyway, with that bad leg of his we could catch him at a leisurely stroll."

"Unless he steals a horse."

A weird little smile turned Penric's lips. "I think such a ride could prove strangely unlucky for him. Don't fret yourself, Oswyl. He may be the best-guarded prisoner you've ever taken."

Penric sounded a bit full of himself on this point to Oswyl's ear, but there were also the three temple guardsmen now being variously distributed with bedrolls between their room and the doors. And the shaman was plainly exhausted. The real danger might well come later, as he regained strength and balance. Oswyl shook his head and followed Penric up the stairs.

Although the bedchamber to which Gossa conducted them was a tidy-enough refuge, no room in this house was spacious. Now containing a washstand, wardrobe, bed, pulled-out trundle bed, bedroll, three men and two large dogs, it seemed even smaller. Gossa handed Oswyl the taper, pointed out the brace of candles on the washstand, bade them goodnight, and shut the door upon them. Oswyl improved the lighting somewhat when he lit the candles, although not the smell, as they were tallow.

Penric politely yielded first turn at the washstand to Oswyl. The prisoner came a pointed third. The sorcerer, who moved like a cat in the shadows, also preempted Oswyl's intent to assign beds by plumping himself down on the trundle, and the dogs capped it by nosing Inglis to the bedroll and disposing themselves to either side of it. Inglis lowered himself awkwardly, with a pained grunt. Oswyl would have put the sorcerer on the floor in front of the door, and the prisoner between them.

"So, Inglis," Penric began. "I am something of a physician, although not presently sworn to practice.

I think I might do a little for that leg of yours, if you'll let me have a look at it."

"Is that wise?" asked Oswyl, startled. To him, Inglis's injury had seemed as good as a leg-iron.

"Oh, yes," said Penric cheerily. "We've destroyed enough fleas in this household to balance a *week* of healing." He glanced at Inglis, made a brief wave of his hand, and added, "And lice."

Inglis, sounding stung, said, "I slept in some vile inns. And I haven't had a chance to bathe properly for a month."

All right, he *sleeps on the floor,* Oswyl revised his plan. And then wondered if Penric had misunderstood him deliberately.

Inglis scrubbed a hand through his ragged hair, then swallowed a startled oath. In this light Oswyl couldn't see the rain of dead bugs, but he could hear the faint patter as they hit the floorboards.

Fluidly, Penric slipped to Inglis's right side, shoved Blood out of the way, and sat cross-legged. Inglis eyed him in doubt, but did not object, though he winced when Pen rolled up his trouser leg. The limb was impressively empurpled and swollen. The sorcerer hummed tunelessly to himself as he ran his hands up and down it. The rigidity of Inglis's body eased. "Oh," he murmured, sounding surprised. Penric's face was bent over his work, but Oswyl could see his lips twitch up.

"A little ragged crack in one bone, but it's not propagating despite your abuse of it. The rest is pulled muscles and some very unhappy tendons. The usual instruction would be to abandon ambition, put your leg up, and rest for about three weeks."

Inglis snorted. Oswyl frowned.

"Indeed. But I may be able to supply a few more treatments as we go along, to replace some of that." Penric straightened his back. There was no visible difference in the leg, but as Inglis sat up in his bed-roll, Oswyl was reminded of those nursery stories where the hero removed a thorn from the wolf's paw and was rewarded with the beast's trust. Did Penric and Inglis know those tales, too? From the wry cast to Inglis's face as he watched the sorcerer, Oswyl thought he might.

Penric added casually, "Did the Old Weald shamans have much in the way of healing arts or practices, do you know?"

"It is believed so." Inglis shrugged. "They were largely lost with the rest of their histories. Most sha-manic teaching was by word of mouth, mentor to aspirant, and died with its possessors. What little was written, the Darthacans burned, if they could find it. What was hidden fell to the worm and rot and lack of understanding. One of the tasks that the fellowship of the royal shamans has set itself is to try to recover those skills."

"Are they making any more progress, in this new generation?"

"Mm, it seems the women tribal shamans worked the bulk of healing practices. They either wrote less, or were less recopied, as most of what survives tends to tales of spirit warriors and battle magic, and the rites surrounding the hallow kingship."

Penric—or was it Desdemona?—vented an ironic snort. "No surprise there."

"The hints are maddening, cast-away remarks in the midst of accounts about greater matters. There is a small cadre of royal shamans working to try to recreate the skills, relying less on old tales and more on new practices. The skills must have been developed in the first place by such trial and error, after all. Except that error…is a problem for an Easthome city shaman in a way it could not have been in the old forest tribes." Inglis had straightened up during this recitation, growing more animated, as if briefly

forgetful of his woes. "A couple of the senior shamans have attempted healings of animals, to try to
get around that. Some of their recent results have
been very exciting."

It came to Oswyl that the reason Inglis had possessed such luck passing for a poor scholar at those
inns was that he *was* one. Well, perhaps not poor.
And Learned Penric was another, officially even.
Two of them. Dear gods, help me.

"Is the Mother's Order taking an interest in the
work?" asked Penric.

"Some, yes."

"Helpful, or hostile?"

Inglis's lips twitched in dark appreciation. "Some
of each, but since the fellowship hit upon the idea of
becoming physicians to animals, their oversight has
grown more favorable."

"Does this work interest you?"

Inglis slumped again. "What does it matter
now? I *can't.*"

"Back when you could," said Penric, blithely
ignoring this burst of despair, "how did you go
about it? How *do* you go into your shamanic trance?
Meditation, medication, smokes, bells, smells...?
Songs, prayers, twirling...?"

Something not quite a laugh puffed Inglis's lips. "All of that, or any. My teachers said they are training aids, to form habits, and so, arbitrary. Nothing *forces* it. Or works like a machine, without fail. The more senior shamans make do with less and less, and some without any. Slipping in and out of the plane of symbolic action as silently as a fish swimming, and seemingly with as little effort." His sigh sounded suspiciously like envy. Or loss, perhaps.

"So how were you taught? Exactly? I have a professional interest in such things, you know."

Oswyl wasn't sure what Penric was about with this line of inquiry—the divine was proving more slippery than he'd seemed at first—but Inglis appeared to accept this at face value. Which said something about Inglis, right enough. But the shaman was going on.

"We always began each training session with a short prayer."

"To invoke the gods, or to placate the Temple?"

Inglis stared at him. "Invoke? Scarcely."

"Yes, everyone talks to the gods, no one expects them to answer. ...Almost no one. Then what?"

"After some experimenting, we settled on a chant for my doorway. It seemed to me the most portable possible aid. And it could never be lost, like objects, or not be around when I needed it. Master Firthwyth first taught me in call and response, like two bards sharing the lines of a long poem back and forth. Except mine was short, just a quatrain. We sat across from each other, with a candle burning between us for me to stare at, and just repeated it over and over. And over and over and *over*, till my mind grew calm, or at least so bored I could scarcely bear it. We went through nearly a box of good wax candles. I worried about the waste. I can't imagine how Firthwyth endured.

"After several days of this, one afternoon when I'd been at it so long we both were hoarse, I...broke through. To the plane. Just for a few moments. But it was a revelation. This, *this* is what I, my wolf-within and I, had been straining for all this time. All the descriptions in *words* I'd been given weren't...weren't false. But it was like nothing I'd imagined from them. No wonder I'd been unable to reach it.

"After that, it quickly grew easier. We dispensed with the candle flame. It took less and less time to break through, and then I began reciting it all by myself. I was working on doing so silently when..."

Inglis broke off. He added lamely, "My teacher said I was good."

"So what's it like for you? To be in this spiritual space."

Inglis's lips parted, closed, thinned. He turned his hands palm-out. "I can give you words, but they won't teach you any more than they did me. I don't know if you can *understand*."

"Inglis." For such a gentled tone, it was oddly implacable. "From the strangest hour of my life, on a roadside four years ago, I have been sharing my mind with a two-hundred-year-old demon with twelve personalities speaking six languages, and an underlying yen to destroy everything in her path, and I expect to go on doing so till the hour of my death. Try me."

Inglis recoiled slightly. And Oswyl wondered at what inattentive point on this journey Penric had started seeming *normal* to him.

Penric sighed and came about to another tack. "Is it intrinsically pleasurable, this trance state?"

"It is a place of wonders." Inglis hesitated. "Some find it fearful."

"And you?"

"I was exhilarated. Maybe too much so." Inglis frowned. "The material world does not *vanish* from my perceptions, but it is…overlain, set aside. Non-material things appear as material ones, symbols of themselves, but not just hallucinations, because in my wolf-form—I appear there as a wolf, or sometimes a hybrid between wolf and man—because I can *grasp* them. Manipulate them. Arrange them to my will. And in the material world, they are made so.

"This does not move matter in the world, not the way chaos demons can, only things of the mind and spirit, yet mind and spirit can have strong influences on the body that bears them. The mind that moves the matter is the mind that is *affected*. A shaman can convince a person to perform an act, or bind two minds together, so that one person knows where the other is. Persuade a body to heal faster, sometimes. Give visions to another shaman, share thought. At full strength, move a sacrificed animal spirit to another body, bind it to that body's nourishment. Animal to animal, to build up a Great Beast. Or animal to…to a person, to share its fierceness…" He faltered. "Making a spirit warrior was considered the most challenging of all rites, apart from the transfer of the hallow kingship itself, and is presently forbidden."

So, it wasn't just the Father's Order who would be wanting a word with this young man when Oswyl returned him to Easthome. It sounded as though his assorted authorities were going to have to get in a line.

"At the sty, for the first time, I made the entry-chant work unvoiced. I was so excited, I almost lost the way again. Since I take the form of a wolf, things usually come to me in a sort of, of symbolic wolf-language. The spirit of the sacrificed boar and the spirit of a kin Boarford were already in sympathy. I chased them like a hunt even as Tollin was struggling to get his knife in, till they superimposed and became one. And then I came down and then...oh gods..." Inglis buried his face in his hands. Arrow whined and licked at him, and Blood rolled over and rested his head mournfully on his knee. Automatically, Inglis reached down and stroked the silky fur.

"Enough of that," said Penric firmly. Inglis gulped and looked up. Penric wrapped his arms around his knees and regarded the shaman through narrowed eyes. "Maybe what you need..."

Inglis and Oswyl glowered at him in equal bewilderment.

"Is sleep," Penric finished. "Yes. Definitely that. Go to *bed*, Penric." He uncoiled and picked his way to the trundle, blowing out the smelly candles on the way.

That was Ruchia, Oswyl thought. He recognized her pithy style, and then was a little appalled that he could now do so. But the advice was certainly sound.

"We need to talk," Oswyl murmured to Penric as he settled down just below him in the darkness.

"Yes, but not now. Tomorrow morning. I need to think." Penric pulled up his covers. "And, the white god help me, compose. Only Mira of Adria was a poetess, and she spoke no Wealdean, apart from some rude phrases she learned from her customers. She was a famous courtesan, did I ever mention that? Now there are your bedtime stories. Although not ones for the nursery. Well, we shall contrive." He flopped over, and whether he closed his eyes, Oswyl could not make out.

Inglis, Oswyl decided, could not get out without tripping over a dog. The darkness pressing upon him like a blanket, he, too, slept.

XI

IN THE GRAY dawn, a bleary Inglis sat up in his bedroll and begged Penric, "Let me blood my knife."

Pen eyed him dubiously. "You've done this every day? All through your flight?"

"Yes."

Was this necessary? Tollin's ghost was surely still lingering, if in an odd form, wrapped around the knife like fine wool on a woman's distaff. And no more faded than Scuolla's spirit, sitting sadly on its rock. *And no less faded, either.* Penric was extremely curious to witness the inner working of this shamanic rite. *Opinions, Des?*

I am out of my reckoning, here. Ruchia's shaman never demonstrated more than the weirding voice in front of us, small help though it was to him. His other enthralling skills were entirely human. If, perhaps, informed by a superior perception...

Pen cut off what promised to be a lengthy, if ribald, reminiscence. It seemed he was on his own for this judgment. "Very well, then."

Oswyl, halfway through shaving at the basin, turned around, folded his razor and stuck it in his trouser pocket, caught up his short sword from where it had stood propped by the head of his bed, grabbed Pen by the arm, stepped around a dog, and hauled him out into the narrow hallway, shutting the door firmly behind them. He drew Pen along to the head of the staircase, and whispered in a furious undervoice, "Are you mad? You want to hand him back a weapon, *that* weapon? Which is also vital evidence, may I remind you."

"It's more vital than that. He's not lying about the knife. It does anchor Tollin's spirit." And an uncomfortable itch in Pen's perceptions it was, Tollin's not-quite-yet-sundered soul held so close to his heart. "Once I watch him through this, I'll be sure of a lot more."

Oswyl's glare heated. *"Scholars,"* he said in a voice of loathing. "You would dangle your arm in a bucket of adders, just to see if it was true that they bit."

Pen's grin flicked, quickly suppressed. *"Once* I've seen, I'll know if it's true he must do this daily to sustain Tollin. In which case you're going to have to let him do it every morning all the way back to Easthome, as routine as washing his face or shaving."

"I'm not letting him have a razor, either."

Pen sobered. "That, I would agree with. Nevertheless, I would ask you to stand prepared for any sudden moves."

"Quite. Sorcerers aren't immune to steel, I understand."

"Actually, Des has a clever trick for that, though I still don't understand how she can equate steel to wood." And this was one knife he most certainly couldn't let her change into a puff of rust in a heartbeat. "But I think Inglis is more likely to turn the knife on himself." As Oswyl's scowl failed to shift, he added, "I can't think you'd be any happier explaining the suicide of your prisoner than you would his escape."

"Much less," Oswyl bit out.

"There's more. If we lose him, through escape or escape into death, I suspect Tollin can't be sustained, and any hope for Scuolla is lost as well. And Inglis's soul hangs in the same balance. They are like three men roped together on a glacier. If the last man can't hold the other two, all will perish in the crevice together."

Oswyl, the lather drying on half his face, thought this over. "I don't see how Inglis can rescue anyone if he doesn't have his powers."

"Neither does he, but I have an idea or two in that direction."

"Five gods, you don't imagine to restore them?" said Oswyl, exasperated. "That would be worse than handing him knife, razor, and dogs together. Why not a saddled horse and a purse of gold, while you are about it?"

"Haven't got a purse of gold," Pen said primly, and was rewarded with the sight of the half-shaved Grayjay baring his teeth. "Besides, in any country so well supplied with precipices as this one, a man doesn't need special tools to end his woes." By his expression, this, too, was a picture Oswyl would have preferred to live without. "As for those dogs... I'm still thinking about those dogs."

Stiff with reluctance, Oswyl followed Pen back into the bedchamber.

"All right," said Pen, dropping down cross-legged on the bedroll in front of Inglis. He reached back and untied the thongs, sleep-snarled with his queue. After pulling out a few fine hairs, he fished the sheath from his shirt, laid it in his lap, and drew the blade. It was a lovely piece of the armorer's art, all lethal curves, capped with old gold and blood-red gems. He held it out hilt-forward to Inglis. "Do what you must."

Inglis took it gingerly, as if he expected Pen to snatch it back like some child's cruel game of keep-away. The dogs on their bellies crept up to either side of him, like furry buttresses. His hand spasmed as it closed on the ivory hilt, and Oswyl, standing over them all with his sword drawn, twitched. But Inglis only rolled back his sleeves and looked his arms over.

Pen stared too. There was scarcely a patch of skin unmarred by red scars, brown scabs, or sticky red lines, with angry pink welts of flesh puffing up between. Double that for the trip back to Easthome, and the man would be flayed. Inglis found a bare spot and lined up the edge, and Penric thought, *Des, lend me Sight.*

The trembling blade sliced, skin split red, and Pen's teeth twinged in sympathetic echo. The view was not much different from his unaided vision, except that Inglis's welling blood bore a strange silver sheen, like moonlight rippling off a wolf's pelt. He stropped the knife up and down, coating every inch. The spirit-wool moved with it, trailing smoke that circled back and settled on the blood. Pen tried not to think of flies swarming on carrion. But the spirit did, indeed, seem to draw nourishment from the strange feast, its density thickening as the blood dried and the silver sheen died.

No, indeed. I don't think our blood would serve the same, murmured Des. As Inglis's fingers started to clench again, Pen leaned forward and wrapped his hand around the shaman's. "I'll just be having that back now. For safekeeping."

After a brief moment of tension, Inglis let his fingers grow slack, and Pen pried the hilt out of his grip. Oswyl waited sword in hand, not yet standing down.

Inglis choked out, "Don't sheathe it till the blood is fully dry. It won't take long. The brown rubs right off with a cloth."

"Right," said Pen, and waited. The trailing smoke seemed to withdraw into the main body of the bound spirit. The sticky turned to crumbly, a few passes on the thighs of Penric's trousers brushed it away, and he slid the gleaming steel out of sight again. Des let the vision of Tollin's ghost disappear, a debatable relief.

⟡

BREAKFAST WAS a quieter meal, as the house's children had not yet returned, although the servant girl had. The six guests, or five guests and one prisoner, were fed on oat porridge with butter, cheese, barley bread, and autumn apples. The dogs loitered lazily by the doors, not enticed by the meatless repast. Conversation was desultory and practical. But Gallin and Gossa seemed very aware of Inglis, and not as a criminal.

Penric had to agree, Inglis had made a terrible criminal. His heart wasn't in it at all. Whatever visions of heroic capture of a villain had beguiled Pen on the ride here, the event had been sadly disappointing. *Though if stupid panic is what's wanted, there's your man,* muttered Des.

I doubt I would have done much better, if I'd killed my best friend by mistake with my new powers, Pen thought back.

*I wouldn't have let you. Nothing remotely like that has happened to a rider of mine...*Des seemed to hesitate. *For a very, very long time.*

Your argument nibbles its own tail, I think?

Humph. But she settled again.

The guard sergeant asked Oswyl, "Should we prepare for the road, sir? We need to see to securing an extra horse."

Oswyl set down his spoon and sat back. "If we can do nothing more here, we should depart, yes."

"You are most welcome to stay longer," put in Acolyte Gallin, with studied emphasis. "A day or so more will not matter."

"Thank you, Acolyte, but I must disagree. Every day we linger risks us being caught by the next snow."

Pen disagreed with both. Might a day or two more here make all the difference, to some?

Gallin bit his lip. "Learned Penric, I would like to speak to you apart. About some Temple matters that concern me."

As a Grayjay, Oswyl was just as much a servant of the Temple as Penric or Gallin, but he permitted Pen to be abstracted from the table with no more than a dry glance Pen's way. The guards looked alarmed to be thus deprived of whatever magical protection they imagined Pen to be providing them, but even if Inglis, Pen didn't know what…weirded them all to sleep and hobbled off, he wouldn't even be able to get as far as the stable before Pen caught him again.

Gallin took Pen to his parlor-study and closed the door, gesturing Pen to sit. When they were knee to knee, he lowered his voice and said directly, "I prayed for help. Are you it?"

Pen sighed unease. "If so, no One has told me. I do not suffer prophetic dreams." He would add, *Thank the gods*, but that seemed to fall under the heading of what his mother had used to call *coaxing lumps.*

"Still, the gods are parsimonious, they say."

"I understand your drift, I suppose. A Grayjay who hates to be late has arrived at the last hour, bringing me, just in time to intersect a shaman who was running away. One need not be delusory to think *something* is expected of us." If Inglis had been in command of his powers, the shaman's role would be obvious, but then, if he'd been in command of his powers, he could have cleansed Tollin's soul on the spot back at Easthome, and be doing, well, who knew what who knew where by now.

Pen's own role so far reminded him of those caravan guards mustered in a mass not to fight off bandits, but to dissuade them from attacking in the first place. Which, he had to admit, was by far the best imaginable use of a force of arms.

"Are Inglis's powers truly broken, as he claimed?"

Penric hesitated. "His powers appear to me to be intact. Only his guilt and distraught mind seem to be blocking his full access to them."

"Can you do something about that? With your powers?"

"The natural directions of my skills are to mar, not to mend. And they work on things, not minds. Mainly." And Inglis's worked on minds, not things. A peculiar reciprocity, now that Pen considered it.

Gallin's fingers pulled at each other. "Then perhaps it's not your skills as a sorcerer that are wanted, but your skills as a divine. Perhaps you are the one meant to give him spiritual counsel?"

Penric was taken aback. "That…wasn't a subject I spent much time on at seminary. It's a rather horrible joke, if so."

Gallin half-laughed. "That's no proof it wasn't from *your* god. More the reverse."

And so the facetious brag he'd made to Oswyl, about being a divine five-fold, curled back to bite him now. Of all the tasks he'd imagined undertaking on the Grayjay's wolf-hunt, whether as sorcerer or bowman-hero, *sage counselor* wasn't even on the list.

So, murmured Des. *Now we see why you are so quick to leave your braids in your saddlebags.*

That wasn't it! he began to argue back, and stopped. He raised his face to Gallin's again. "You've served here for many years. You knew Scuolla, as a friend and as a shaman. Surely you must be better fitted for such a task?"

Gallin shook his head. "Friend, yes, I hope so. But I can't say as I ever understood what he did with his dogs, except to observe that there seemed no malice in it, or in him. But you and Inglis kin Wolfcliff, you are both brothers in the uncanny. You see things veiled from me. Maybe you can see the way out of this tangle, too."

Penric cleared his throat, embarrassed. "I admit, I had an idea or two. But it was just for things to try. Not any kind of *wisdom*. Oswyl thought it high foolishness, in fact."

"Locator Oswyl wants to leave, I gather. Can you not overrule him?"

"The princess-archdivine assigned me to him, not him to me. The task was his to start with before it grew"—Pen hesitated—"so complicated."

"Could he hold Inglis without your aid?"

"Well..." Penric reflected on the possibilities inherent in that weirding voice, were it to be deployed without restraint. Not to mention the other shamanic skills. "No."

"It seems you are the linchpin in this wheel, then. If you elect to stay, he cannot take Inglis and go."

"That...would seem to be the case, yes."

"Then I beg you to stay. And apply your ideas. Or counsel. Or wisdom, or unwisdom, or whatever you may dub it." Gallin drew breath. "You have to *try*, at least."

Pen imagined a prayer, or a holy whine—to the white god, either would do—*If You don't like it, give me something better.*

The silence in his head was profound. Even Des did not chaff or chatter.

Penric managed a nod. Trying not to let his doubts show, he returned to the breakfast table to shepherd Inglis—and the two dogs—back to their bedchamber.

THEY SETTLED cross-legged facing each other on the bedroll once more. Blood flopped down across the doorway and sighed; Arrow sat up beside Inglis and appeared to watch with more than canine interest.

"All right." Penric took a breath. "What I'm going to do here is give you a clean new chant to gate your entry into your spirit space."

Inglis shot him a stare of surprise and offense. "What makes you think you can do the first thing about it? Sorcerer."

"I'm the one who's here. That seems to be the most vital point at present." Refusing to wilt under Inglis's frown, Penric forged on, "My call shall be, 'Father, Mother, Sister, Brother, Other.' And your response shall be, 'Bless this work and let me serve another.'"

"Is that supposed to be the blessing?"

"No, that's your chant. I thought I'd combine the two and save steps."

Inglis met his bright smile with a deepening glower. "It's a stupid rhyme."

"I'm a sorcerer, not a poet."

"Evidently. It's not even a quatrain."

"Repeat it, and it will turn into a quatrain."

Inglis looked ready to rebel. Or at least to refuse to cooperate. And what Penric would do then, he had no idea.

Des muscled into brief control of his mouth, and said in honeyed tones, "Or you could pray, 'Other, Mother, Father, Brother, Sister. Thwack my head and make me less a blister.'" Pen failed to control the upward crook of his lips as she fell back.

After a long, black silence Inglis said, "Use the first one."

"Good," said Pen. And a firm, *No more interruptions now*, to Des. She settled back, falsely demure. "I'll begin. Father, Mother, Sister, Brother, Other..."

They began to repeat the call and response much as Inglis and his possibly-not-that-long-ago mentor had. The mindful if simple (*or simple-minded*, Des put in) prayer really did grow boring after enough repetitions. A while after that, the syllables began to lose any meaning or connection at all, a steady, soothing double drone. Pen did not let up until both their tongues started stumbling, when he called a break.

Nothing had happened. Well, he hadn't expected it to, Pen lied to himself. All right, he'd been *hopeful*.

"How often did your shamanic master repeat your practice sessions?" asked Pen.

"It varied, depending on his duties and mine. Sometimes, once or twice a day. Sometimes dozens."

"And how long did you drill at a time?"

"Much as now, till our tongues grew too tired to fruitfully go on. That, too, varied."

"Hm." Penric slapped his knees and stood up. "Rest your tongue, then. And your leg."

Inglis at least did not argue with this injunction.

Pen found one of their guards seated at the top of the staircase. "Where is Oswyl?"

"He walked over to the temple, I think, sir."

"Thank you." Penric threaded his way through the house and turned onto the street. The temple stood as quiet and dim as yesterday when they'd surprised Inglis inside. Once again, the hall held only one supplicant. Oswyl sat upon his knees before the altar dedicated to the Father, tucked up against its one-fifth portion of the wooden walls. His head turned at the sound of Penric's steps.

"Oh. It's you."

"Don't let me interrupt," said Pen. And then, incurably curious, asked, "What do you pray for?"

Oswyl's lips thinned. "Guidance."

"Oh? I thought everything we've encountered here shouts our course at us. Or are you just angling for a different answer?"

Oswyl turned back toward his chosen god's altar once more, the very set of his shoulders sturdily ignoring Pen.

Pen walked to the hall's opposite side and studied his god's niche. The shrines here had a profusion of woodcarvings, common in country temples in this region. On the lintel, the carver had placed a well-observed flight of crows; in a lower corner, some earnest-looking rats. The Daughter's shrine, to Penric's right, was decorated with an explosion of wooden flowers and young animals, painted in their proper colors, a muted glow in the shadows. A supplicant prayed *before* a shrine, Penric's teachers had made clear, not *to* it. He lowered himself to his knees. Emptying his mind was not an option, but he didn't need to badger the gods, either. He waited.

After a while, Oswyl's voice came from across the hall: "Did you get anywhere with your tutoring?"

Not turning, Pen answered, "Not yet."

A wordless grunt.

After a little, Pen said, "He's not really a murderer, you know."

A pause: then, "My task is to bring a fugitive to justice. Not to judge him."

"Yet you must use your judgment. You followed your own line on the Crow Road."

A considering silence.

"I have another trial in mind," Penric continued. "I want to take Inglis out to the rock fall, and see what he can make of old Scuolla." And what Scuolla would make of him?

A mere pained sigh was all that this elicited. What, was he finally wearing Oswyl down? It occurred to Penric that Oswyl was not so rigidly rules-bound as his stiff jaw suggested; only doubt need pray for guidance. He hoped Oswyl would get his answer. Penric went on speaking to his own wall: "Inglis is in less pain than yesterday. Calmer, if not less bleak. I expect I should take Gallin. And the dogs. We'll need one of the guardsmen's horses. Do you wish to come? Given you've no hand in the uncanny."

Oswyl's voice returned, distantly, "Having spent this long and come this far to find him, I'm not losing sight of him again."

"Well, then." Penric bowed his head and signed the tally, and they both rose together.

XII

*I*NGLIS, TO HIS chagrin, had to be helped onto his horse by two guardsmen and an upturned stump by the stable door. His stick presented another puzzle. He finally set its butt upright atop his foot, which also had to be fitted into his stirrup by a guard, and held it like a banner pole. That and his reins seemed to give his hands too many things to do. The sorcerer almost floated up into his saddle, although Inglis put it down to his wiry build and horsemanship, not magic. Acolyte Gallin availed himself of the stump, however. Given the acolyte's age, that was small consolation. Locator Oswyl frowned down from his mount at Arrow and Blood, swirling amiably around Inglis's horse; the horse, which Inglis judged something of a slug, took only mild exception.

Gallin led the mounted party out past his temple into the street, where Learned Penric held up a staying hand. "Let us go to the bridge, first," said Penric to him. "And over it. I want to see something."

Gallin shrugged and turned his mount left instead of right. The rest of them followed in a gaggle. The dogs, who had darted ahead in the opposite direction, paused and vented puzzled whines. When the riders continued their retreat, they barked a few times, then ran after.

As Penric made to lead them all across the wooden span, Arrow and Blood rushed ahead, turned, and set up a furious barking. The horses shied.

"Calm them," Penric advised Inglis.

"Hush!" Inglis tried, and then, "Sit!" The apparently-maddened dogs continued to hold the party at bay. **"Hush!"** Inglis tried again, more forcefully. **"Settle down!"**

The two dogs recoiled as if blown by a gust of gale, but then remustered their battle line and took up their din again, standing four-legged and braced, the fur rising in a ridge along their backs.

"Enough!" cried Penric, laughing for no reason that Inglis could discern, and made a twirling motion with his fingers. Gallin, staring back and forth between the dogs and him, reined his horse around to lead back up the vale once more. A few villagers arrested by the uproar who had come to their garden gates nodded at their acolyte, frowned impartially at his visitors, and turned back to their interrupted tasks.

The two guardsmen fell in at either side of Inglis, albeit not too close, scowling at him in distrust. Oswyl nudged his horse up beside the sorcerer's, and asked, "Did you do something, back there?"

"No," said Penric, airily, "not at all. Very carefully not at all, in fact."

"So what was all that in aid of?"

"I had three theories about what drives those dogs. This knocks out one of them. Two to go." He nodded in satisfaction, and pushed his horse into a trot after Gallin. Oswyl seemed as baffled by this as Inglis, for he made an exasperated face at the sorcerer's retreating back. What, did the locator find the blond man as irritating as Inglis did?

A little while later Penric reined back beside Inglis, displacing one of the guards, who looked more grateful than otherwise for being relieved of his post. "Well," said Penric cheerily, "shall we beguile the ride with a bit more practice?"

"*No*," said Inglis, mortified. And if a **No!** would have worked on the man, he'd have followed up with one. "Do you want us both to look fools?"

"That still concerns you, at this stage in your career?" Penric inquired. Entirely too dryly. "Though I have to allow, working for my god tends to knock that worry out of a person fairly swiftly." The dryness melted to an even more excoriating look of sympathy.

"I don't know what you're planning, but it's not going to work."

"If you don't know the first, how do you know the second?" Penric shot back. "Although I'm afraid planning may be too grandiose a term for it. Testing, perhaps. Like the bridge."

Inglis hunched his shoulders. Penric eyed him a moment more and then, to his relief, gave up.

The day was gray, the air damp, the mountains veiled, but the wind was light, not spitting rain or snow at them. Inglis studied the vale as they rode up the right-hand branch of the Chillbeck. The high peaks at its head, and easterly, led only to more peaks. One would have to circle back several miles to find any western trail with even a chance of leading to a high pass over to the main Carpagamo road. It was a half-day's ride downriver beyond that to loop south to the same road, the way Inglis had come in. Given his prior disastrous experience with trying to climb out over this valley's walls, that seemed the best bet. If a man had a head start on a fast horse. The notion of trying to retrace his route all the way back to the Crow Road and head east to Saone after all, as winter turned from threat to certainty, was near-heartbreaking.

The riders strung out as Gallin turned off the road and up into the woods. The sorcerer rode right behind Inglis, a thorn in his back; one of the guards went ahead, looking frequently over his shoulder. The woods were difficult but not, Inglis thought, impassable. Centuries of valesmen gathering deadfall and timber from these more accessible lower slopes had left them semi-cleared, although tangled steeper ravines and erupting granite rock faces broke up the area into a maze.

At length, the trail opened out onto a fearsome-looking landslide, much larger than Inglis had been picturing, and the riders pulled up. The two dogs scampered ahead onto the debris.

Penric peered out over the waste after the bounding animals, and asked Inglis, "What do you see?"

"When I am not in my trance, my sight is the same as yours. Er, as any man's." This was not quite true in this moment, Inglis realized. There was a breathless pressure in his mind, as if he were plunged deep underwater. A shiver up his spine. Tollin's spirit, wound around the knife under the sorcerer's shirt, was so agitated Inglis could sense its hum from here. "What do you see?"

"When Des lends me her vision, I can see the spirits much, I think, as saints are said to do, matter and spirit superimposed, like seeing both sides of a coin at once. Scuolla seems a colorless image, like a reflection on glass. I see he's changed his rock since yesterday. So he can move about, some. May be a trifle smudgier? Or maybe that's what I expect, or fear, to find." Penric's gaze had alighted where Arrow and Blood circled a boulder, whining. "He's looking over at us. At you? He perceives us on some level, certainly. If you could—when you could—achieve your trance, did you see spirits? And could they speak to you, or were they silent?"

"I'd not encountered many. The old ones were always silent. I'd not evoked a new one yet."

"Tollin."

Inglis winced. "Tollin is bound to the knife, and does not speak. To me. In my normal mind. I don't know if…" He trailed off, confused. If he could have ascended to the spirit plane, might they have spoken together despite the binding? Inglis wasn't sure if he would have raged at Tollin for this disaster, or begged his forgiveness, or what. If he had lost a friend in more ways than one, or if some peace might have been salvaged between them, at an hour beyond the last. If Tollin hated him…

Penric, Oswyl, and one of the guardsmen dismounted, the latter taking the reins of all three horses. All of Gallin's attention was on the dogs. The second guardsman kicked his feet out of his stirrups, preparing perhaps to go to Inglis's aid. The sorcerer's bow was still bundled with his quiver, unstrung, tied to his saddle. For the first time in weeks, the burden of the knife was taken out of Inglis's hands.

If ever I am to have a chance, it is now, right now.
Inglis threw back his head and **HOWLED**.

Every horse in the party reared in panic and bolted, including his own. He tossed away his stick, wrenched at his reins, and managed to get the beast aimed generally uphill. They plunged into the patchy forest. From behind him, curses and a thump as someone fell off, more curses fragmenting as a man still mounted was carried away back down the trail. For a few moments, all Inglis could do was hang on to his saddle and reins as the animal under him heaved and jinked. He bent low as slashing branches tried to behead him, sweep him from his precarious perch.

Uphill and to the left was his goal—circle around the top of the slide and lose himself in the lower forests, then find his way somehow back out of this trap of a valley...the stolen horse was essential, crutch to his bad ankle, he couldn't let it break *its* legs here...at this pace it must grow winded soon, and then he would regain control...

He had reckoned without the dogs. They gave chase, barking and baying behind him, weaving faster through the trees than the horse could. Incredibly soon, he saw a rippling copper flash at the corner of his vision, and, already *above* him, heard the profound deep barks of Arrow. They began to drive his horse through the tilted woodland like a red deer, hunted, and its laboring haunches bunched and surged in fresh terror—his fault, for filling its

dim head with visions of wolves, echoing and rever-
berating now from the dogs? But a deer was built
for these hazardous slopes; a horse was not.

A gulf of light opened to his left, and the horse
shied wildly, hooves slipping in the wet loam, almost
stumbling over the cliff at the top of the slide. It
jerked back upright.

Inglis kept going, the saddle yanked from under
him. The world whirled wildly around his head. For
an instant, the bed of broken boulders far below him
invited him like a bed in truth, an offer of rest at the
end of an impossibly long day. A branch brushed
his arm, and his hand closed convulsively, unwilled.
Bark and skin grated each other off like bits from a
blacksmith's file. Wood snapped, he turned again in
air, grasped, arm yanked straight, held, slid, lost it,
turned, and smacked hard on his side. If he'd had
any breath left, the last impact would have knocked
it out. His lungs pulsed and red murk flooded his
vision before he was at last able to inhale again.

It was a dozen breaths before he could lift his
head and see where he'd landed. Raw stone blocked
his vision a foot from his nose. He twisted the other
way, and looked out over the gray valley. He'd come
to rest on an irregular ledge about halfway up the

sheer drop at the head of the rockslide. It was deeper than a kitchen chair, but only just, and several paces long, but they were paces that led only out into air at the ends.

No way to climb back up. No way…well, one way down. He eyed the broken rocks fifty feet below him, and wondered if the half-fall would be enough to kill him outright. Certain death still held attraction. Uncertain death, less so. He hurt enough *already*.

The skin of his hands was torn, his shoulder wrenched, his bad ankle…not improved. Spectacular bruises for sure. Amazingly, his neck and back and bones generally seemed intact.

Fifty feet above him, piteous whines sounded. A few barks, less labored or frantic than before—more puzzled yaps, really. *Whatever are you doing down there?* they seemed to say.

Truly, I have no idea. I have no idea about anything anymore.

He lay on his ledge and concentrated on breathing, achievement enough.

After a time, he became conscious of movement below him. He pushed himself a little up and looked over. The drop reminded him of crawling out on the roof of the kin Boarford's Easthome city mansion, five floors above a cobbled street—Tollin had dared him, he recalled. The pale face of the sorcerer looked up at him, head back-tipped. Penric was breathing fast, but otherwise seemed unfairly unruffled.

He shook his head, and called up, "I swear, Inglis, you have a talent for disasters. ...It's not a *good* talent, mind you. On the other hand, I'd suspected you had help, and now I'm sure of it."

Inglis could go neither up nor down, right nor left. He felt as exposed as a wolf pelt nailed to a stable door, and as empty. He could think of no reply, not that the sorcerer had invited one, exactly.

A hundred paces away across the scree, where the path had been cut off, Gallin cupped his hands around his mouth and shouted, "Baar caught a horse! We're going for ropes!"

Learned Penric waved a casual hand in acknowledgment of this news, a lot less excited than Inglis thought he should be. "That will be some time," he said, half to himself—the over-keen hearing that had come so disconcertingly with his wolf-within had still not deserted Inglis. Penric skinned out of his heavy jacket, turned up the cuffs of his linen shirt, rolled his shoulders, stretched his arms and laced his fingers together, shook them out. "Well, then," he muttered. "I decline to shout spiritual counsel from the bottom of a well, so I guess I'd better be about this."

He flattened himself to the cliff wall and began to climb, barely visible handhold to barely visible foothold.

His mouth opened, and his voice emerged in a strained, sharp cadence Inglis had not yet heard from the man: "Penric! I have many powers, but I can't make us *fly!*"

Penric grinned, fierce in his strain. "Then you'd best keep quiet and not interrupt for the next few minutes, eh?"

At a distance, at first, he seemed to scale the rock face like a spider. As he grew closer the illusion dropped away, and he was clearly a man, taller and heavier than he had quite seemed in his smiling affability; the tendons stood out in his hands and arms as he pulled himself up. As he gained each few feet he wheezed, "I admit...it's been...a while..." When he at last reached the edge of the ledge, he very definitely heaved himself over, scrambling, not like the airy aplomb of vaulting on his horse. "Thank you, Drovo," he gasped, incomprehensibly, rolling to his knees, shaking out his hands again. "I think."

Slowly, gingerly, Inglis pushed himself upright and scooted back till his spine met the stone. His outstretched feet hung over the abyss. Breathing heavily, Penric plopped himself down beside him and stretched his legs out, too. They might have been two boys seated side-by-side on a log across a stream. Perhaps feeling the same, Penric picked up a loose stone and tossed it over the side, cocking his head as if listening for the splash. The faint crack of its landing was a long time coming.

Pinned crookedly to the left shoulder of his weskit, Inglis saw, where it had lain concealed beneath his coat, the divine sported the Temple braids of his full rank, three loops of interlaced white, cream, and silver, the hanging tails tipped with silver beads. They were stiff and clean, as though seldom worn since Penric had taken his oaths. That could not have been so many months before Inglis had been invested with his own powers. Penric's ceremony had probably had less blood in it.

Although, considering the necessary origin of his demon, not less death, nor a lesser sacrifice. *Hm.*

Oswyl's voice called from the rubble below: "Is he all right? Or were you prophetic about precipices?"

Penric swung around on his belly and hung his head over the edge, a move which made Inglis shudder. He did stretch and crane till he could just make out the locator, standing below looking up as Penric lately had.

Penric waved back. "Seems to be little the worse. Shaken up, though."

"Fools and madmen," Oswyl muttered, and sat down on a handy boulder, heaving an exhausted sigh. A bigger man, he did not seem inspired to hoist himself up what Inglis had taken for a sheer rock wall after the divine. Sorcerer. Whatever he was. He raised his face and voice and added, "Remember what I said about putting him on a horse?"

Penric grinned, and called back, "Remember what I said about the luck of such a ride?"

"Huh." Oswyl grimaced like a man sucking vinegar. "Carry on, O Learned One."

"I intend to. Is he not what every Temple divine desires, a captive audience?"

"I still want him back when you're done with your lessons."

"Pray for us, then."

The gesture Oswyl made back at this was not in the least holy. Penric, still grinning, spun around and sat back up, and Inglis's spine sought the reassuring rock again.

The grin faded to a thoughtful look, and Penric began to edge away, then stopped himself. "Scuolla has joined us," he said quietly.

"Is that"—Inglis's hands went to his temples—"why I feel this horrible pressure in my head?"

"Did you hit it, in your fall?" A look of medical concern flitted across Penric's features, and he leaned across the space to lift his palm and press against Inglis's forehead; Inglis flinched.

"Not much," said Inglis, as Penric murmured, "No..."

His hand falling back, Penric went on with maddening obscurity, "Then I think it must be your other visitor."

Inglis uncompressed his lips, and said, "What does Scuolla look like? To you?"

Penric stared at the empty space between them. "A plain old mountain man in a sheepskin vest, rudely interrupted when he went out to feed his animals. Not at all what I would have taken as a great-souled one, beloved of the gods. Lesson to me."

"Great-souled? I thought that was kings, and, and generals."

"No, those are merely great men." Penric kept on gazing curiously at nothing. "He is very patient. Well, he would have to be, wouldn't he, to work his art in a medium that takes more than a man's lifetime to complete. ...Another who waits here is not so patient, I think." The pressure in Inglis's head throbbed; the divine made the five-fold tally. "So let us pray, too."

"Pray? Are you serious?"

Penric turned his hands out in a shrug. "It's my job. My other job, I was lately reminded. From my very first oath, three years before these"—he touched his braids—"were tacked on me."

"So what do we pray for, ropes? Pulleys?"

"Such material aids are the purview of men, not gods." He held up his hand and spread out his fingers. "The five theological purposes of prayer, I was taught, are service, supplication, gratitude, divination, and atonement. You could easily go five-for-five up here, I think." He dropped his hand and smiled faintly out over the valley; the dreary view did not seem to rate such approval.

"What do *you* pray for?" Inglis thrust back, growing surly with this elliptical...humor, if it was humor. At his expense, of course. He was feeling entirely destitute, just now.

"I try not to bother the gods any more than I can possibly help," returned Penric, unperturbed. "Once, One answered me back. It was an experience to make a man cautious."

"Twice, I think," growled Inglis.

"Hm?"

He leaned his aching skull back against the stone and recited, "Other, Mother, Father, Brother, Sister..."

Penric's lips twitched. "Are you feeling, ah, thwacked?"

"If I were any more thwacked right now, I don't think I could sit upright." Inglis sighed. "You go right on being stingy with your prayers, Learned."

"Let us practice yours some more, then."

"Will that be any safer?"

"I trust not. Begin. Father, Mother, Sister, Brother, Other..."

Their recent drill made his reluctant response fall inevitably: "Bless this work and help me serve another." He eyed the empty space Penric had left between them. Had the couplet's wording not been so simple and silly as he'd thought?

"Continue on your own."

"Father, Mother, Sister, Brother, Other..."

It was foolish. He was a fool. So was Penric. They were all great fools, here. He should just give up and live with the fact. The other choice was the rock bed, which had already killed one shaman, which could cap a lifetime of foolery. Did the gods take fool souls, as well as great ones? No, They couldn't, for the fools ran away. Gods, but he was tired of running away.

As the fifth repetition left his lips, he broke through. As sudden and astonishing as his very first ascent ever, he was *there*. But this time he could hold his place, like a falcon gripping the air and, miraculously, rising without even beating its outstretched wings.

The ledge, the stone behind and the vale in front, the material world, were still present, but barely, as a great undefined space seemed to open out all around him. Undefined, yet seething with potential. But he was not alone in it.

Sitting next to him indeed was an old mountain man in a sheepskin vest, his feather-decked hat pushed back on his head. He wasn't an image on glass, though, but full of color, vastly more intense than the faint gray valley around them. His spirit-density was the very opposite of transparent. The beautiful Great Dog he bore within him had made its home in this kennel for so long, the two were nearly one, intertwined. He smiled in a friendly way at Inglis, with a strange pure kindness unalloyed by irony or judgment. He didn't even seem to say, *You are very laggard*, though Inglis thought he had a right.

Penric sat beyond him, staring head-tilted with concern at Inglis's body. The blond man's solid self was grayed out as well, along with all the other surfaces of the world, but for the first time Inglis saw under the sunny exterior. The sorcerer's *interior* was terrifying, its layered complexity reaching back through time like a cavern passageway descending deep into the earth, dark with secrets. His demon. *And he lives with this? Every day?*

Then he looked up, farther.

A tall figure leaned casually against the ledge wall beyond Penric. It seemed a young huntsman in the poor men's dress of this country, much like the fellows who had brought Inglis in off the trail that first morning, or like Scuolla. A triangular sheepskin cap topped his glowing copper curls, which were the color of Blood's fur. His face was a light much too strong to look at directly, and Inglis shaded his spirit-eyes with his spirit-hands, then clapped them over his face altogether. All else was blocked, but not the burning light. He let his hands fall, and found himself gasping as though he had been running.

He thought the face smiled at him, like the sun through the cool air on a mountain's side, warming, welcome. And far, far more terrifying than the demon.

The figure waved a casual hand. *Go on.*

"How, lord?"

Call it out of him. For you, it will come. It was a very good dog, after all.

It couldn't be that simple. Could it? *Here, it can. This is a simple place, after all.* And Inglis wasn't even sure whose thought that was.

Inglis inhaled the no-air of the plane, held out his hand as if to a strange dog to sniff, and called, **"Come, boy."** Then felt stupid for the trailing endearment, for surely the beast was far older than he was...

Stop that, said the figure's voice, amiably, like a man commanding his pet to stop scratching. *This is the time for my judgments, not yours.*

The response was slow, like an old dog or an old man getting up, one-half at a time. Stiffly, but obediently, the *shape* flowed out of Scuolla. Slipping through Inglis's hands, like a whisper of fur as a dog wriggled out of his grasp. And gone. Where? Surely not into utter dissolution?

"Will it be well?" Inglis asked timidly.

All will be well, in my hands. But you see now why all hunts, however exciting, must end with respect for the creature hunted. That is your hope, too, after all.

Inglis had no idea what to say to that. In terror lest the figure would vanish again, as if—no, he neither summoned nor dismissed this like some mere apparition, but he blurted, "Lord, there is one other."

I do not forget. But that is your task, now.

At some point, Penric had drawn the knife from its sheath and held it ready on his lap. He squinted in concern at Inglis's body, still sitting up against the rock wall: more motionless than sleep, too tense for death. With a huge effort, Inglis flopped out its hand, open. Cautiously, Penric laid the knife on its palm. The hand convulsed around the ivory hilt; Penric quietly lifted hand and knife back into Inglis's lap.

For the first time, Inglis realized he had appeared on the plane in his human form—not as wolf, or even as man-with-wolf's-head. It might be a good thing. The stretched-out boar spirit was, he saw now through its ferocity, quite frightened enough. This time, he coaxed it out softly, gently. He had hated it for what it had done to Tollin, and through Tollin to himself, but it was one of the Son's creatures with the rest. He handed it off to the waiting god, and bowed his head in respect, and spread his fingers wide over his heart in His sign.

Tollin unwound from the knife and stood up, looking dizzied and bewildered. His colors were ragged, paler than Scuolla's, who sat taking it all in like a satisfied onlooker to some beloved campfire tale. Tollin's mouth opened as he saw Inglis, though no sound came out, but then his face rose to the figure by the wall, and he stood stunned.

For a moment, to Inglis's horror, Tollin held back. Guilt, grief? Fear of not being good *enough*, strong *enough*...it had not just been youthful arrogance that had led him to beg for the boar spirit, after all. A mixture of motives not savory, but so, so understandable to Inglis now. Tollin stood silent, and small, and ashamed.

The Son of Autumn held out His hand, close but not touching. Tollin's face turned away, suffused with misery, but his hand jerked out, once, twice. On the second, his hand was grasped, and all anguish fled from his features, because the astonished awe left no room for it.

And then he was gone.

The Hunter turned then, bent, and extended his hand to Scuolla. Who, to Inglis's surprise, spoke, and in the affectionate voice of a man to a long-time comrade: "But will there be good beer?"

The Hunter's voice returned, in like humor: "If there is beer, it will be very good. If there is not, it will be because there's something better. It's not a wager you *can* lose. Come on, old man."

As the Hunter heaved Scuolla up, the old man said, "You took your time, getting here."

"I did My best with what I had," the god answered him back.

"Seems so." Scuolla looked warmly down at Inglis. "Take good care of my dogs, lad."

Inglis nodded, breathless. "I will, sir."

Scuolla dipped his chin in pleased acceptance. "*Now* I can go."

"About time," his Friend murmured, amused. "Who is dawdling now?"

Inglis found himself on his knees, holding up both hands palm-out, fingers spread. He hardly knew what he meant to say. *Is that all, am I done?* Instead it came out, "Will we meet again?"

The Hunter smiled. ***Once, for certain.***

And then Inglis let go, and he was falling, falling, back into the world, laughing so hard he was crying, or crying so hard he was laughing, or some other reaction much too large for any human frame to hold.

Fortunately, Learned Penric was waiting to catch him before he rolled off the ledge that he'd forgotten was before him.

"There, there..." Penric clutched his shaking body and patted his back as if calming a hysterical child, prudently dragging him over to the wall again. "You've seen a god, I know, I know," he soothed. "You'll be drunk on it for days. No doubt Oswyl will be highly offended, which will be entertaining in its own way..."

Gasping, Inglis rolled over in his lap and grabbed up at his collar. "*What*, what did you see? Just now?"

Penric gently undid his clenching fingers before he tore the fabric. "I saw you go into your trance. It was a bit alarming. Might have been taken for a stroke—you should warn your companions about that. Your nose bled. I saw when Tollin came unbound, and when he went off. Scuolla, too. It was hard to get much more, because Des went into retreat. Since she has nowhere to go but inward, this results in her curling up into this sort of impenetrable, *useless* ball—" his voice rose on this last, not, apparently, to Inglis's address, for he added aside to Inglis, "Gods terrify demons. They are the one power that can destroy them. Understandable." Inglis wasn't sure who was supposed to understand what, but Penric hesitated for a long moment. He held up his hand, fingers spreading as if miming a man pressing on a glass, except that it also recalled his five kinds of prayers. *Supplication*, Inglis thought. "Otherwise...otherwise, it was like standing outside a window in the rain, looking in on some harvest party, to which I knew I was not invited."

"Oh," said Inglis, stupidly. And at an echo in his mind of *Stop that*, grinned uncontrollably despite it all. He rubbed at his upper lip, and his hand came away sticky and red, but the bleed seemed to have ceased on its own.

Penric held his hair and peered down into his face with a curiosity...medical? theological? magical? or just the inquisitive scholar? Voices and barking echoed from below, and Penric craned his neck. "...Right. So, here comes Gallin, and a lot of excited men with ropes. I hope they brought enough. Arrow and Blood are running over to greet them, or maybe hurry them along. Or trip them and break their legs, hard to tell with dogs. Are you going to give us any *more* trouble?"

"I am in your hands," Inglis said, limply. And truthfully. And thankfully.

Rescue. *I am rescued.* Of all men to be lost in these mountains, he had to have been the most lost, and the most rescued. Such rescues had been Scuolla's calling, had they not? him and his brave band of dogs. The shaman's last rescue, and the shaman rescued, hand to hand to hand to hand in a long, long chain of help beyond hope. Reaching how far back?

...And how far forward?

XIII

ETTING THE TWO men off the ledge took over an hour. Like the injured shaman, the sorcerer waited to ride the rope net down; unlike the shaman, he stepped out of it with the panache of a prince descending a palace stair. When taxed by Oswyl, Penric claimed that it was much harder to climb down than up, because he couldn't well see where he was putting his hands and feet. No mountaineer, Oswyl had to take him at his word. It was hardly a thing to balk at, considering what all *else* of the uncanny events he was forced to take the sorcerer-divine's testimony for. The eager Acolyte Gallin ate up their wild tale like a starving man, and asked for seconds. The guards and the valemen grew wide-eyed. In all, it was rising dark before they made it back to Linkbeck once more.

Inglis, certainly, seemed a man profoundly changed, unless the fall had struck him mad. Madder. When they'd cleaned up, and Penric in his third guise as physician had seen to their prisoner's new bruises, they all went down to dinner, where Gallin and Gossa were slavishly grateful—to *Inglis*. For Gossa, this took the form of trying to stuff him like a feast-day goose, and feeding his dogs like people. Penric beguiled his own neglect by telling the servant girl, who turned out to be the daughter of the village wet-nurse, all about the fine opportunities for an energetic young woman in the silk industry at Martensbridge, under the princess-archdivine's careful eye.

Oswyl finally broke it up by announcing an early start in the morning. As they mounted the staircase, he said to Inglis, "You are still my prisoner. Still under arrest. And we are still going back to Easthome."

"Oh, yes," said Inglis, pensively. "It's all very good now. And if it is not, there will be something better."

For his part, Oswyl predicted a blizzard with the dawn.

IN THE blackest hour of the night, Oswyl dreamed.

A deep, slow voice, which seemed to reverberate to the ends of the world, said judiciously: **"You were not too late. Well done, child."** After a thoughtful pause it added, in a far less grave tone, "No snow tomorrow. But do not linger three days."

Oswyl, scrambling to sit up, came awake with a cry. He didn't know if the sound was night-terror or joy, but it was loud.

Dogs yipped, covers were thrown back, and Penric's voice out of the shadows called, "Des, lights, lights!" He then cried in fear, "He'll burn my eyes!" and replied to himself, "You haven't got eyes. I do and they're just fine. Or they would be if there were any *light* in here. *Thank* you," he added, as upon the washstand the two tallow candles sprang into flame all by themselves.

Oswyl, clutching his blankets, gasped, "He... He..."

"Are you all right?" asked Penric, concerned. "You sound like a horse with the heaves."

"Nothing. Nothing," Oswyl managed, trying to catch his stolen breath. "Pardon."

"Judging from Des's reaction, it was not *nothing*." He added, "You can come out now. I think it's over." He twisted around to Inglis, who was sinking sleepily back into his bedroll and coaxing the dog Blood to lie down to be clutched like another pillow. "Did you sense anything, just now?"

"No...I don't think it was meant for me." He cuddled the dog, which slowly gave up its alert mien and put its head on its paws once more. Arrow stepped over, and on, Penric in his trundle—provoking an, "Oof, you enormous beast! Paws off!"—and stretched his damp black nose to sniff curiously at Oswyl.

"It was just a dream," said Oswyl. "Maybe, maybe a little hallucination. It's been a long day." And a long, strange chase.

"A bad dream?"

Oswyl hardly knew, except the corners of his mouth kept crooking up, unaccustomed and unwilled. "No... It was...a different kind of frightening." He added, "How can you tell? Discern a true voice from, from a mere dream?"

"If you need to ask, it was a mere dream. The other is rare but, hm, not as rare as you'd think. Our daytime minds, I'm told, are too full of ourselves to let Them in. Well, and mine's too full all the time. At night our gates come sometimes ajar, just enough."

Oswyl's brows drew down. "That's…unhelpful."

"What was your message?"

He wasn't embarrassed, exactly. But… "I'd rather not say. It would sound too absurd."

Penric, propped up on one elbow, studied him thoughtfully. He finally said, "A bit of free theological advice. Do not deny the gods. And they will not deny you."

As Oswyl stared at him, he went on, "Dangerous habit, mind you. Once you start to let Them in through that first crack, They're worse than mice."

Oswyl, thoroughly bemused by now, protested, "How can you speak of the gods so irreverently? And you a full-braid divine?"

Penric shrugged a half-apology. "Sorry. Seminary joke, there. We had a hundred of them. Needful at times of stress. One of my masters said, For all that we trust the gods, I think we can trust them to know the difference between humor and blasphemy."

"Not so sure about *your* god," Inglis's voice came from his bedroll.

"Hey. Yours is no better. A god whose harvest of souls includes all whose last words were, 'Ho, lads!

Hold my ale and watch this!' …Seminary joke," he added aside to Oswyl, who hardly needed the gloss.

Inglis snickered into his dog, and then mused, "That would be funnier if it weren't so true."

"If it were not true, it wouldn't be funny at all."

The two young scholars seemed willing to debate the theology of humor, or the humor of theology, till dawn. Oswyl said loudly, "You can snuff the candles back out, now. I'm all right."

Penric smiled at him, eyes narrowing. "Ye-es. I expect you are."

"Want to borrow a dog?" Inglis offered. "They're very soothing."

"In my bed? No, thank you."

Arrow, snuffling over the edge of Oswyl's blankets, heaved a disappointed sigh, as if finding that the source of some delicious scent had gone.

"What," said Penric, "they don't have fleas—don't everyone rush to praise me. And Gossa made her children wash their paws."

"You are welcome to him," said Oswyl, shoving the beast back into the trundle. "You, go sit on your master." Giving up on his riotous company, Oswyl struggled from his bedclothes and went to blow out the candles himself.

THE HEAVY snow did not close in till after they'd reached the safety and warmth of Martensbridge, three days later.

XIV

AT THE KNOCK on his workroom door, Pen looked up from his calligraphy and said, "Come."

The door swung open cautiously, and a palace page entered. "The Temple courier has brought you some letters, Learned."

Pen set his quill in its jar and turned to accept them. "Thank you."

The girl ducked her head and, after a last curious look around, went out again.

Penric examined his take. The thinner missive was marked with a Temple stamp from the Father's Order in Easthome; the larger, wrapped in a piece of old cloth and waxed against wet, had been franked by the Wealdean royal court chancellery. He opened it first, to find a letter and an unbound book, freshly copied and pristine. Both from Inglis, ah.

It had been over a month since Oswyl and his prisoner, and his prisoner's vigorous pets, had departed for Easthome. Penric had managed to evade being taken along by virtue of the week they'd all spent snowbound in Martensbridge, which had allowed him to scribble out a full deposition of the late events in Chillbeck Vale, heavily slanted in Inglis's favor. Normally a trip to the Wealdean royal capital at the Temple's expense would have been a high treat, but—not in midwinter, despite Oswyl's descriptions of the fine Father's Day festival put on there at the solstice. *Not my season.*

Nor mine, sighed Des. *Did I ever tell you about the sun on the sea around Cedonia?*

Several times. He'd never seen a sea, warm or cold. Could a demon be homesick? Pen wondered, and broke the seal on Inglis's letter.

Inglis thanked him for his deposition, which had done the trick—the shaman did not appear to be writing from a condemned prisoner's cell, certainly. *You were right that the god-drunk wears off,* Inglis wrote, *for I was very sober when we reached*

Easthome. I have been strongly reprimanded by the Royal Fellowship, and put on probation, whatever that means, but not dis-invested. I am not sure anyone can actually do that, or at least, no records of such a skill have surfaced in the ancient annals. It seems the old method of execution for bad shamans was to hang them upside down and drain them of blood, which no one in the Fellowship has suggested even for the experiment.

The Father's judges after much debate finally ordered me to pay a fine to Tollin's family, in the old style, by way of weregild. My parents had to borrow some of it from our kin lord, which did not please anyone very much, but I trust they'd have been less pleased to see me feet-up with my throat cut. Oswyl says I should just give up on Tolla, but I am not so sure. She did listen to my tale and mark my scars. Tollin's second funeral was a comfort to his family, I think, though redundant, as I saw very well which god took him up, and told them so. I'm not sure some believed me until their local temple's holy animal signed Autumn at his graveside.

I had a copy made for you of the Fellowship's writings on shamanic practices that you wanted to read, at least as they are understood so far. I hope we'll need a second volume in a few more years. It seems small *thanks, but it was what I could do. You should find it under seal with this letter.*

He signed it with a flourishing *Inglis kin Wolfcliff, Fellow of the Royal Society of Shamans (on probation).* And added, as a cramped postscript at the bottom of the sheet, *The dogs are well, and settling into their new home. We maintain a bit of a menagerie here, so they fit right in. They like Tolla.*

Penric's fingers itched to dive for the new volume, but he opened the thinner letter instead. As he'd hoped, it was from Oswyl.

You may be pleased to learn that your affidavit was accepted by the court, though immediately afterward seized upon by some theologians and carried off. From the legal side of things, there is no sign that anyone wants you brought here in person after all. The other I cannot speak to. Inglis got off lightly, but I do not feel there was injustice done.

My former sorcerer and his party arrived back at Easthome about two weeks after we did, frostbitten, footsore, and empty-handed. Happily, their official complaints of me were stopped by word of my success. Their private ones, I feel no need to attend to.

I set an offering on your god's altar the other day, in Temple.

His signature was neat and square, *Oswyl, Senior Locator, the Father's Order at Easthome.*

He, too, added a cramped last word: *I am not sure how demons feel about blessings, so please just give my best wishes to Desdemona.*

Des was so astonished, she was momentarily silent.

Penric smiled and reached for his new book.